KU-618-934

BAINTE DEN STOC

WITHDRAWN FROM DÚN LAOGHAIRE RATHDOWN
COUNTY LIBRARY STOCK

Soul of the Border

MATTEO RIGHETTO

Soul of the Border

Translated from the Italian by Howard Curtis

PUSHKIN PRESS

Pushkin Press
71–75 Shelton Street
London WC2H 9JQ

Original text © Matteo Righetto 2017
English translation © Howard Curtis 2018

Soul of the Border was first published as *L'anima della frontiera*
in Italy by Mondadori in 2017

First published by Pushkin Press in 2018

Published by agreement with Piergiorgio
Nicolazzini Literary Agency (PNLA)

1 3 5 7 9 8 6 4 2

ISBN 13: 978-1-78227-465-0

All rights reserved. No part of this publication may be reproduced,
stored in a retrieval system or transmitted in any form or by any
means, electronic, mechanical, photocopying, recording or otherwise,
without prior permission in writing from Pushkin Press

Quotation from *All the Pretty Horses* by Cormac McCarthy © Pan Macmillan,
reproduced with permission of the Licensor through PLSclear

Author photo © Giacomo Giovanni Stecca

Designed and typeset by Tetragon, London
Printed and bound by CPI Group (UK) Ltd, Croydon CR0 4YY

www.pushkinpress.com

To the free, the just, the poets, the saints:
spirits without borders

He thought that in the beauty of the world were hid a secret. He thought that the world's heart beat at some terrible cost and that the world's pain and its beauty moved in a relationship of diverging equity and that in this headlong deficit the blood of multitudes might ultimately be exacted for the vision of a single flower.

CORMAC McCARTHY,
All the Pretty Horses

PART ONE

1

THERE ARE VILLAGES that smell of misfortune.

You just have to breathe in their air to recognize them, air that is murky and thin and defeated, like all things that have failed.

Nevada was one such village, with its handful of men and women living in hovels that clung to the steep slopes on the right-hand side of the river, hovels half-hidden by ragged woods and scattered here and there among the *masiere*: those little terraces, reclaimed from the mountainside, that descend towards Enego to the east of the Asiago Plateau, and then plunge into the Brenta and Sugana Valleys.

It was on these *masiere*, demarcated by walls built up from the chipped stones that spring from that earth in greater profusion than moles, that the locals grew tobacco. They had been doing so for generations, for centuries, because there above the Brenta Valley tobacco grew well and was of better quality than any other in circulation, which was why it had already replaced the timber trade by the seventeenth century, at a time when down in the valley, from north to south, bubonic plague was raging and it seemed as if there was no future for anybody.

2

As the nineteenth century drew to an end, only three families lived in Nevada, and one of them was the De Boers.

Augusto was the head of the family. He was born in 1852, when his land was under Austrian rule, in the same house he would live in all his life and to which he would bring his wife Agnese, the daughter of peasants from a place called Stoner: four houses clinging to the Asiago Plateau. With her he would have three children, two girls and a boy, all born in Nevada, in that very same house.

Augusto was not a tall man, nor was he bulky, but he was endowed with surprising, inexhaustible strength. With five blows of an axe, he was capable of felling a spruce twice his age. He had a thick black moustache that concealed his mouth, which was often busy chewing tobacco. He spoke so little that often he was silent for days on end. Whenever his lips moved, all conversation around him ceased. His words were as final as tombstones.

He had grown up in poverty, narrowly avoiding pellagra, and had seen dozens of men and women, including his father and mother, survive the hunger and famine that had beset the mountain dwellers over the years.

That might have been why Augusto De Boer felt the burden of responsibility on his shoulders and lived every day in the full awareness that the fate of his family, for good or ill, was linked to his, like the branches of an oak to the trunk.

That was why he thanked God twice a day, in his way. He did it when he got out of bed with the first song of the thrushes and set off to work on the *masiere* and when he returned in the evening, bones aching with fatigue. Then he would eat a chunk of polenta and little else, arrange the firewood in the stove and go to bed.

Lying in bed with his eyes closed, he would listen to the song of the nightingales out there in the woods and feel a burning pain in his back from the day's labours.

3

AGNESE WAS THREE YEARS younger than him and had never been back to Stoner since leaving. Her hands were stubby, the skin red and chapped on the back, the palms covered in little cracks. She always walked fast, as if in a hurry, with her head down. Few people had seen her hair: once black, it had turned white suddenly, and she wore it swept back into a bun and hidden under a dark kerchief tied under her chin.

She prayed a lot, even when she worked in the fields or stirred the lumpy, ochre-coloured polenta in the pot. She prayed above all to the Virgin Mary. Some summer days, she would return home from the *masiere* so tired that she did not even have the strength to eat, and so she would make dinner for the others and sit down by the stove or else on the steps outside the door, and there she would rest, moving her lips in a long prayer. She was a sensitive soul and, despite the strain of living at these heights, she was amazed and enchanted every day by the beauty of nature's little things: a dandelion, a hazelnut, a jay's multicoloured feather. She had never received any gifts, and she wished for nothing, except to see her children grow up healthy and good Christians.

4

AUGUSTO AND AGNESE had three children. Jole was born in 1878, Antonia in 1883 and Sergio in 1886.

Physically and emotionally, Jole was just like her mother, which was probably why she loved her father above all. She almost always tied her blonde hair in a long plait that fell between her shoulder blades. She was thin and had large, bright eyes of indeterminate colour: at times they seemed as green as a larch grove in summer, at others as grey as a wolf's winter coat, at others still as blue-green as an Alpine lake in spring.

More than anything else, Jole loved horses and even as a little girl walked barefoot through woods and down impracticable paths just to see them. To satisfy her passion, especially in summer, she was capable of leaving in the morning and not returning until just before sunset. There were two places where she could see them: to the north, on the pastures of Rendale, where there were many nags that followed the shepherds and their Foza sheep, and to the south, on the ridges of Sasso, where a large number of carthorses were used to transport marble from the quarries.

She liked all horses, whether they were light-footed stallions or heavy farm animals. As a child she would look at them in awe, her big eyes open as if to capture a dream, a piece of magic.

Her sister Antonia liked to wear her hair short, and Agnese cut it for her twice a year with old iron scissors, taking care not to prick her because tetanus was less forgiving than hunger. Antonia would help her mother in the house, and she liked making things to eat with what little there was. She, too, was often in the woods during the summer. She went there to listen to the cries of the wild animals and smell the pleasant aromas of the trees.

She would gather in an old tin can the resin secreted from the bark of the spruces and take it to her father, who would knead and mould it into hard little balls, useful for lighting the fire in the stove. Augusto, though, would always leave a little for Antonia, who used it to protect flowers or particularly beautiful insects from the ravages of time, thus adding them to her collection.

But Antonia did not only gather resin. She also gathered wild strawberries, raspberries and elderflowers, with which her mother made an excellent, refreshing juice, mixing it with water from the river.

It was the big river down in the valley that was the favourite spot of the youngest of the De Boers. Often Sergio would walk through the wood that stretched to the east of Nevada and sit down on the edge of the cliff over the Brenta Valley, and from there look down and listen to the sound of the river as it descended towards Bassano del Grappa and then, further still, on to the Venetian plain. Sergio was skinny and fair-haired. He was never still. Of all of them he spoke the most and was never quiet for a second. As a joke, his mother and his sisters always said he spoke double the amount because as well as his own voice he had also assumed his father's.

All three children, though, apart from living their days with the ardour, the dreams, the blessed unawareness of every little girl or boy of their age, worked hard in the tobacco fields alongside their parents: it was a fate that nobody was allowed to avoid.

5

THE DE BOERS lived as best they could—in other words, they survived, like any mountain dweller in those years, or indeed at any time.

In the last few decades, both down in the Brenta Valley and on the vertical slopes of the plateau on one side and Mount Grappa on the other, hundreds of families had abandoned the land to seek their fortune, some going as far as the other side of the world.

The De Boers, though, had remained there, growing tobacco for one king or another, struggling bravely with a life of poverty and sacrifice. Nostrano tobacco from the Brenta was highly regarded, grown both for snuff and for smoking in several varieties: Cuchetto, Avanetta, Avanone and Campesano. But to obtain a good product required a great deal of work. It was a long and delicate process: a single mistake could compromise the entire year's crop—and that, for peasants, meant starvation.

The work began at the end of February, once the harsh winter was over, with the preparation of the ground for digging. Armed with hoes, Agnese, Jole, Antonia and Sergio removed the *rega*—the weeds—lining it up in bundles, and spread the manure. At the beginning of March, they set about digging furrows, moving the clods further uphill to prevent the earth, because of the slope of the terraces, from bearing down on the lower *masiere* and risking a landslide. The digging both eliminated the *rega* and improved the structure of the soil.

By the end of this first task the furrows ran through the plots like railway tracks. The real digging began towards the middle of May, and this was a rapid operation. It was a task that fell to Augusto and, of all the tasks, was the hardest. As it was impossible to use the plough on these steep, narrow fields, the ground had to be prepared by hand. The spade turned over the clods of earth and smoothed them with great skill, guided by Augusto's toil and sweat.

Thus levelled, the ground was ready to welcome the little shoots of tobacco. Then Agnese and her children began sowing them in the *vanede*—the small beds specially prepared in a place sheltered from the wind and exposed to the sun—while Augusto made the ground ready. It was at this time every year that the representative of the Royal Tobacco Company came to Nevada to deliver to the De Boers the fifteen thousand seeds necessary to equip the seedbed. To calculate the number, he would use a measuring cup no bigger than a thimble.

On Maundy Thursday, Agnese would go down to the river and wash her face as a sign of penitence and purification, then come back up to Nevada with two buckets full of water and give a few drops to each new shoot of tobacco. In the first days of June, the transplanting began. Augusto would trace crosses, and in the middle of these Agnese and the children would place the shoots, already ten fingers high, and moisten them with a little of the water brought from the Brenta. When the plants were three hands high, Agnese and Sergio would fertilize them with sludge from the lavatories and remove the weeds and the worms. Those that had gone to rack and ruin were replaced by others, known as *rimesse*: plants that if they were not used had to be uprooted and destroyed in front of the emissary from the Tobacco Company.

But there was still a lot of work to do.

When the plants reached Augusto's waist, they were trimmed. It was Jole who took care of this: she would carefully prune the tops, so as to aid the development of the lower leaves. After this operation, Jole would keep a close watch on them: within a few days the buds would sprout and were immediately removed. It was boring work, which Augusto was happy to delegate to her and Antonia. Then the lowest leaves, which were of little value, were removed before the king's inspectors came to check. Finally, they would wait for September, when the leaves would begin to ripen. At the right time, the whole family would gather them and put them to soak so that they would turn yellow. Augusto and Agnese would place them very carefully in the shed, with their tips turned upwards and their ribs towards the outside.

Of all the family, only Augusto could judge when the leaves were yellow enough. He would examine them one by one, putting aside those not yet ready and sorting the others according to size. He often had to check the correct degree of soaking in order to prevent them from going bad or rotting. The air in the shed at such times was heavy, and it was already clear from the expression in Augusto's eyes whether the quality was good or the year's crop had to be discarded. For days, the De Boer family lived in expectation of a sign from Augusto. When it came, they would all carry the leaves into the loft and lay them on the *smussi*, the wooden planks on which the leaves would dry. After a couple of weeks Augusto would turn the leaves over and lay more planks over them.

The last part of the work was the most prosaic. By now, Augusto would already know whether the tobacco was of good quality, and he would take a few days' rest. He would supervise his family as they sorted the leaves according to size and quality and gathered them into bundles of fifty and tied them with string or, sometimes, with lime-tree bark. Within a few days, the bundles were ready for the Tobacco Company. The final operation, in the open air, was performed by little Sergio and consisted of removing the stalks that had remained on the terraces after the harvest. Once this was done he would beat them together to get rid of the earth and pile them in little sheaves ready to be burnt the following spring.

6

AFTER THE TOIL of the fine season, family life took on a calmer, slower pace during the months of cold. With the approach of winter, movements and sounds and noises both inside and outside the house gradually abated until they disappeared, sometimes for days on end. The life of the De Boers was filled with idle moments, moments of intimacy and boredom. From December to February, it seemed as if the cold and the short days would never pass. They lived a more secluded, almost meditative life, marked out with domestic matters and the obligations that the peasant world and poverty dictated as rigid, irrevocable rules.

One morning just before Christmas 1888, Jole and little Antonia were in the kitchen, where there was a pleasant smell of vegetable and boiled cereals. Augusto was in the shed tending to the animals, and with him was Sergio, who was then not much more than two. Agnese, meanwhile, was outside, shovelling the snow that had already started falling the previous night. To warm herself a little, Antonia settled for a few minutes next to the cast-iron stove. Then she went and stood under the window which looked out on the yard and finally climbed onto a chair and sat in the window recess to watch her mother through the rough, steamed-up pane.

Agnese was not still for a moment. Although the snowfall seemed stronger than a thousand shovels, she continued undeterred to clear both the path in front of the house and the lane that led to the shed, the barn and the vegetable garden, even though in this season there was no longer anything to gather in the vegetable garden.

The surrounding landscape, or at least what could still be glimpsed of it beneath the heavy blanket of low white clouds, was completely covered in snow, and over everything there hung not only a sense of peace but also a sense of being adrift.

"Come on, Antonia, come here!" Jole said to her little sister, taking two eggs and a bowl of milk from the lopsided shelf on the wall. "Give me a hand, the *menestra de orz* is nearly ready!"

With the agility of a cat, Antonia got down from the window recess and then from the chair and bounded over to her sister.

"What shall I do?" she asked.

"I'll beat the eggs and the milk, you keep stirring the soup."

Jole had been watching the pot for more than three hours, regularly shifting it about on the surface of the cast-iron hotplate to make sure it remained at a constant heat and endlessly cramming the stove with medium-sized beechwood logs. Since morning, when her mother had gone out with the shovel in her hand, she had had the task of preparing the barley soup which the De Boers would eat for lunch and dinner over the next two days. Agnese had pre-soaked the cereals the previous evening, when the air was already promising snow but flakes had not yet started to drop from the sky, and in the morning her elder daughter—still only ten but already able to manage in the kitchen—had had to take over.

So, early that morning, Jole had first chopped the vegetables that Augusto had kept cool in the *giazèra*—an icebox dug in the earth—since the summer, then put them to boil on a slow flame along with the barley. Because they were in Advent, which for Agnese was a period of fasting and abstinence, she had not added even a small piece of pork rind.

"It smells good!" Antonia exclaimed, taking the lid off the pot with her eyes closed and sticking her nose in the steam that rose to the ceiling.

Jole smiled and continued to mix the eggs and milk in a wooden dish until she had produced a slightly doughy, whitish mixture.

"Pour a little in my dish!" she said to her younger sister.

"Why don't you put the cream in the pot instead?"

"Mamma says that way it becomes as lumpy as ricotta. You have to do it a little at a time."

That is what they did, after which Jole poured the contents of the dish into the pot and mixed it all together. In a few minutes, the soup was ready and the two girls tasted it with the ladle.

"Oh, my, that's good!" Jole said.

"Very good!" Antonia exclaimed.

They looked each other in the eyes and smiled with satisfaction, conscious that they had a new little secret between them. Then they laughed loudly, like two accomplices who know they have got away with something.

Just then, Agnese came into the house, all sweaty despite being covered in snow from head to foot. She took the kerchief from her head and placed her hands on the side of the *stube*.

"The first snow is good for some things," she said. "The prints tell us if there are wolves around. But it's best to clear it right away, or we might find we can't get out through the door."

Jole nodded, removed the pot from the fire, put five bowls and a piece of old bread on the table and announced proudly, "It's ready to eat, Mamma."

Agnese said nothing. Catching her breath, she looked at her two girls and a big smile lit up her purple face.

"Oh, my, what a smell!" she said finally, with a look of surprise. "My dear little women. Congratulations, Jole. Congratulations, little Antonia. May God bless you both, my girls."

All three smiled.

A few moments later, Augusto came into the house with Sergio on his back.

Without saying anything, they sat down at the table, prayed and ate the barley soup with real pleasure, while outside the winter raged, the snow a bright, blinding white even though it was Santa Lucia, which the peasants said was the shortest day of the year.

This was how the days were, and they would stay this way, more or less, until the following spring.

Regular and repetitive, like the constant succession of saints on the calendar.

7

E VERY YEAR THEY WORKED HARD for little gain. The inspectors of the Tobacco Company came by one last time early in October to collect the leaves and pay off the De Boers with money barely sufficient to feed five mouths for an entire year.

It was genuine exploitation, but there was nothing anyone could do about it. Consequently, in order to survive, you needed to think up something else, and this something had a specific name: smuggling.

The limitations imposed by the Tobacco Company's monopoly were experienced by all the peasants as an undue intrusion by the State into family life—robbery, if not a kind of slavery—and so breaking the law and defrauding the State was a kind of necessity.

When you were a smuggler, you did not become rich, but at least you lived less poorly. It was like making grappa at home, poaching, slaughtering several pigs and declaring only one, killing a calf and selling it without paying the royal duty. Small ploys that enabled you to keep going with more dignity.

In those years at the end of the nineteenth century, if a peasant was skilful and, above all, had guts, he could manage to hide a few kilos of tobacco every year.

And Augusto was very skilful and had a lot of guts. There were three things in particular at which he was clever: growing and then hiding the *rimesse*, the plants used to replace those that had not taken root or had become spoilt for some reason; hiding the lower leaves before the visit of the inspectors; and drying part of the *fior*, the highest and most prized leaves, as quickly as possible. The quickest way to do this was to crush the *manego*, the central venation, with a stone roller or a small wooden hammer. Thus treated, the leaves were left to dry in the sun in inaccessible places hidden from visitors and from the binoculars of the customs officers exploring the cliffs on the right-hand side of the Brenta in search of illegal tobacco factories.

Augusto would illicitly hide the tobacco he managed to extract in a number of secret places: natural refuges, animal lairs, sometimes holes dug with his own hands. In the fields and woods around Nevada, there were at least ten hiding places that Augusto had prepared over the last few years, that is, since hunger had begun to tighten its grip.

Of course, Augusto was not the only one in those parts to smuggle tobacco. There were at least two or three men who transported it along paths and over sometimes impracticable passes known only to them, defying the vigilance of the customs officers. Occasionally they would lose the load, having to abandon it in order to avoid being shot at or thrown in prison. And in some cases, as they escaped, they would slip from a crag and lose not only the precious load but also their lives.

In some families, smuggling amounted to a tradition. They had done it under the Austrians and continued to do it under the Italians. And Augusto did not like either.

The Austrians because they had exploited and then abandoned the Veneto, the Italians because they had taken it and immediately placed it under the yoke of the House of Savoy, depriving the people of their freedom as well as their tobacco. But the main reason he did not like them was that, as far as he was concerned, any ruler was equal to any other and neither Cecco Beppe nor Vittorio Emanuele II had ever taken the trouble to fill the bellies of the mountain peasants. That was why he had always felt himself a stateless person.

But with the passing of time, Augusto De Boer became different from the other smugglers. He was no longer prepared to risk his life to take a little tobacco down into the valley in exchange for flour. And so an idea came to him. Something much riskier but also much more lucrative.

As a boy he had been to Primiero with his grandfather, who was a carter, and had seen with his own eyes that there were a large number of mines there: copper mines, iron mines, even silver mines. And, again accompanying his grandfather to festivals and country fairs, he had been to Bassano and down as far as Cittadella, where he had seen coppersmiths who were always in search of cheap copper with which to make and adorn fine pots and tools of all kinds.

This was what Augusto De Boer thought of doing: smuggling tobacco across the Austrian border and taking it to the miners in Primiero. Tobacco in exchange for metals, especially silver and copper. He had realized that any man in the world would give anything for a handful of fine tobacco, and the miners more than anyone else. And then Augusto would go down into the plain with those metals and exchange them for food supplies and cattle.

And so, at the end of summer 1889, he set off.

He was thirty-seven years old and his children were eleven, six and three. This was the first time, and like all first times it did not prove at all easy. It was an extremely risky thing to cross that damned border and take your chances, defying danger and fate, defying the cholera and smallpox that often infested the valley with the breath of the devil, defying prison and, above all, death.

But if you wanted to survive, the call of the border was stronger than anything else.

8

B Y 1893, Augusto De Boer could boast that he had already made that journey five times, one each autumn. Not that the risks had diminished in any way. On the contrary: the king's customs officers on the one side and the guards of the *Zollwache* on the other had reinforced their patrols, and crossing the border had become increasingly arduous and fraught with danger. Nevertheless, Augusto, who was only forty-one but had a face as forbidding and full of lines as the trunk of an old elm, had managed to plot new paths and devise new hiding places, like a lone wolf chased by hunters and forced to escape to save his skin. He felt strong and was conscious of having accrued a certain wild Alpine instinct, thanks to which he no longer felt any fear. In fact, he took a certain pleasure in challenging the unjust laws of the powerful, their guns and their borders, and in winning that challenge every time for love of his family.

9

"THIS YEAR JOLE is coming, too," Augusto said one summer evening.

He had just finished eating a bowl of bean soup. He got up from the table and went and sat outside the front door, on the rough porphyry steps that looked out onto a meadow and the little vegetable garden and further still, across the *masiere* that spread eastwards as far as the eye could see, all the way to the peak of Mount Grappa beyond the Brenta Valley. The sun was setting on the opposite side, tinging the woods with soft tones of pink and orange that made those wild, rugged places seem welcoming and gentle. After uttering those words, as rough and dry as the bark of an old chestnut tree, Augusto took out a pinch of tobacco, stuck it in his mouth and began to chew it under his thick moustache, in which there were already a few white hairs, savouring it as a cow savours the flowers of a green pasture. His figure seemed small beside the big mountain ash his father had planted beside the house many years earlier, a mountain ash that produced orange-red berries and every year in September was assailed by myriads of robins and tits.

He chewed the tobacco, still staring up at the mountain tops. Between these and his eyes there were a large number of terraces, a sea of inaccessible woods, dark forests, steep slopes and walls of rock. The first fireflies were just beginning to rise from the thickest grass. After sunset, they would become a second firmament, much to the delight of Sergio, who enjoyed capturing a few of them every evening with Antonia's help. From the oak wood came the repeated cry of an eagle owl, followed by the distant howling of wolves.

Then silence.

10

AGNESE AND THE CHILDREN had remained in the house. Agnese was nervous, and the wooden ladle she was using in the kitchen fell several times from her hand. The words uttered by her husband kept going round and round in her head, and she knew there was very little she could do to dissuade him. Antonia picked up the ladle from the floor and gave her mother an anxious, bitter smile, then helped her to rinse in the tub the wooden bowls from which they had eaten the soup. Sergio had heard nothing: when his father had uttered those words, he had been daydreaming, imagining he was flying over the Brenta Valley to see what shape the river was. He thought it must resemble a snake, maybe that long green whip snake his father had captured in the shed just three days earlier.

"This year Jole is coming, too." Augusto had said it just like that, without anyone expecting it and without anyone being able to answer back. Before those words he had been silent for a whole day, and after them it was anyone's guess when he would open his mouth again.

With a gesture of the hand, but also with a stern, frightened look, Agnese made it clear to Antonia that she should take Sergio and go with him to the bedroom. Once they were gone, Jole, too, stood up to leave the room, but her mother intervened.

"Jole!" she cried, seizing her by the arm.

Jole wriggled free of her strong grip but then stood there ready to listen, as a daughter should listen to her own mother.

"If I spoke to him he wouldn't listen," Agnese said. "Just like it's always the oldest stag that gives the orders in a herd of deer, in the same way he's the one who decides. It's the law of nature."

Jole felt her mother's voice turn tremulous and did not dare look her straight in the eyes. She was afraid she might discover a tear on her face and did not want to embarrass her, or to embarrass herself. So she stood there and stared at the wall, but continued to listen.

"I beg you, daughter, try and talk to him. Tell him you don't want to go, that it's too soon, that you're still young. This is men's business. Try and tell him that."

Jole summoned up the courage to turn to her mother, and in her clear eyes all the compassion and anxiety rising from her heart were visible.

"Mamma," she said softly, "the truth is, I…"

"You?…"

"I want to go, Mamma! I want to go with him!"

"Oh, my daughter, what are you—"

"I couldn't wait for him to ask me, Mamma. I'm big now."

"But you're only fifteen, you're… you're—"

"I'm strong, that's what I am. And besides, with my father I'll be safe. He wouldn't take me with him if he didn't think we could do it and he could protect me. I trust him!"

"Who doesn't trust him? That's not the point, Jole. The point is that… that…"

34

Jole embraced her before she could finish the sentence. She clasped her tightly and said, "I'm going with him, Mamma."

At this point, Agnese realized that she had no hope of getting her to change her mind, and so there was nothing left for her to do but yield to that embrace. She clasped her daughter ever more tightly and let the tears stream down her face, knowing that nobody in the world would ever see them.

11

A FEW MINUTES LATER, Jole came out of the house and sat down on the steps next to her father. She smiled at him and clung tightly to his arm, as if it were a rope thrown to a woodman who has fallen from a cliff.

"This year I'm coming, too, Papà."

Augusto closed his eyes to savour even more the tobacco he was moving ceaselessly between his tongue and teeth and palate, and at that moment the noise of the Brenta came to his ears from down in the valley.

A feeble but constant sound that climbed all the way up here, to Nevada, thanks to the stones and rocks over which the water ran its course.

12

THREE MONTHS LATER, the long-awaited moment arrived. Jole was excited and, to ease the tension, spent the evening before the journey playing with Sergio. Equipped with penknives, they carved a spruce log into a dozen little wooden horses. While her brother thought about these horses, she thought of the adventure that awaited her. She could hardly contain her impatience. She realized that it would be risky, but was certain that since she was going to be with her father things would go well. The experience would probably turn out to be the most important of her life.

In the previous weeks, Agnese had objected to Augusto's decision and had tried several more times to dissuade her eldest child—and even her husband—but her words had been in vain.

"Someone else has to learn," he had replied curtly on a couple of occasions.

And so the moment came to leave.

In the week preceding their departure, Augusto had prepared every detail with care and attention. One thing at a time, calmly, leaving nothing to chance. He had collected just the right quantity of tobacco from the various hiding places, weighed it, obtained water, fitted and filled all the bags and cases in which the tobacco was to be hidden during the journey, let the mule rest and feed more than usual, wrapped pieces of cheese—Morlacco, Bastardo and mature Asiago—*sopressa* salami and smoked ham, put dried Lamon beans and Cimbrian potatoes in small jute sacks, taken a two-litre bottle of grappa, checked his and his daughter's boots and dug out two large blankets, two rucksacks, a few ropes, a large wooden canteen, a rough hemp sheet, a lantern and a holy picture of St Martin.

Last but not least, he went to the shed, opened an old oak-wood chest and looked at the two Werndl-Holub rifles hidden in it, excellent Kraut rifles he called "St Peter" and "St Paul", for which he had bartered a fair amount of silver in Bassano the previous year.

13

I T WAS THE DEAD OF NIGHT—more precisely two o'clock on the morning of Monday 29th September 1893—when Augusto De Boer and his daughter set off.

Such was Jole's emotion, she could feel her heart bursting. Her hands were cold and sweaty and moved in an awkward way.

She had got out of bed barely half an hour before their departure, but in truth she had not slept a wink. She had lain awake all night listening out for wild animals, trying to imagine what awaited her in some unknown place at some unknown time, out there beyond the hills that had always marked the limits of her world.

Her father was already up, waiting for her in the shed: four walls of rough stone and old planks of wood, the upper part of which, covered in grass and moss, served as a hayloft.

A few years before, a small wild blackthorn had sprung up in a corner of the roof, probably as the result of a kernel fallen from a redstart's beak. Augusto had decided to leave it there because he liked the idea of having a fruit tree over the hayloft: offering food to the birds, he said, brought good luck. In April the branches filled with snow-white flowers, and in September they were laden with little round purple sloes of which the blackbirds and thrushes and tits were very fond.

Augusto did not want his children to gather these fruits, since he considered them an offering to the birds of the wood, a kind of reward for these frail creatures, a mark of fraternal solidarity.

Agnese and Antonia greeted Jole in the kitchen without lighting any candles: the customs officers might have spotted their nocturnal movements even from a distance. Sergio was unaware of anything and continued to sleep. Agnese gave Jole a cup filled with hot milk and she savoured it a little at a time, taking small sips, thinking about when she would again be able to taste anything like it.

She knew that if everything went smoothly, according to the plans laid down by her father, she would be back home in three or four days at the most, but she knew that even a mere handful of days would seem to her infinitely longer than that.

She donned heavy garments in which tobacco was concealed everywhere, put on her boots, tied her long hair with a length of thick hemp twine, loaded her rucksack on her back and left the house. At the door, her mother and sister embraced her in silence. She summoned up her courage and went to join her father in the shed.

During those twenty steps that separated her from the shed, Jole took a deep breath. The sky was damp and cold, and a light haze brought with it the strong penetrating smells of early-autumn nights, leaving them hanging in mid-air: mist-soaked moss, moulting animals, sickly-sweet late-blooming flowers, shrivelled wild berries, withered mushrooms.

Augusto had already harnessed Hector, as Jole had called their mule, loading him with everything, but above all with tobacco, in addition to the tobacco that father and daughter were keeping hidden in their clothes and shoes and ankle bandages. It was sealed within dozens of pockets, cavities, compartments and internal pouches, invisible to any possible search.

That year the harvest had been good and Augusto had somehow managed to hide almost a hundred kilos, in various forms: pressed leaves, shag and powder. There was something for every taste and every vice.

The two exchanged glances in the darkness of the shed, the whites of their eyes the only things that glowed in the dark. In the enclosure, the hens clucked drowsily, annoyed at being disturbed. Jole stroked the cow, Giuditta, one last time, then walked out and waited for her father to join her.

Her hands were still cold, her movements still awkward. Her heart began beating even more loudly than before, and the persistent smell of manure penetrated her nostrils as if trying to cling to her breathing, to travel with her and be with her for the whole journey.

"Let's go," Augusto whispered, slinging the rifle called St Peter, already loaded, over his shoulder, next to his rucksack, and so saying he closed the door of the shed. They slowly passed the vegetable garden and came close to the door of the house. There, Agnese and Antonia approached like two shadows to bestow their final farewell. Agnese embraced her husband, then put a red kerchief around her eldest child's neck. Antonia kissed both of them.

Nobody uttered a single word.

The two of them set off. Augusto walked in front of the mule, holding the reins and leading the way, and Jole followed a few paces behind. They walked slowly, moving away from the house towards the steep path that slipped down into the woods beneath the walls of rock and led to the valley and the great river.

Antonia ran back into the house, perhaps so as not to cry, whereas Agnese mustered the courage to follow them with her eyes until the last moment, until they were swallowed like ghosts, first by the night fog, then by the dark forest of broad-leaved trees.

Her Jole was fifteen, Agnese thought, no longer a child but not yet a woman. She prayed to the Madonna for her and for her man. At that very moment, Jole took from a pocket a little wooden horse, one of those she had carved the previous day with her little brother.

"I'm a real *smuggler*," she whispered into its wooden ear.

Then she hugged it to her chest and felt less afraid.

14

THE PATH WAS SLIGHTLY MUDDY, with a thin layer of dew, and the dampness of the night had softened the ground and made the backs of the stones slippery. Once they had moved into the heart of the woods, Jole and her father had to be careful not to slip and fall.

All at once, she took a few steps forward and had to rest a hand on the mule's back to avoid losing her balance.

It is always strange to begin a journey downhill.

She would have liked to say something, ask her father how long it was going to take them, but she remained silent.

Over the preceding weeks, Augusto had told her that they should speak as little as possible during the journey. The customs men were hiding everywhere, you should never be too trusting, not even when you thought you were safe.

Remembering these words, all Jole could do was think about what she would have liked to ask him and try to find the answers to her questions for herself.

Augusto immediately set a gentle, steady pace, although the descent was gradually becoming more difficult and dangerous because of the steep drops that loomed suddenly at the sides of the trail.

Soon the path contracted even more, until it was as narrow

as the mule's belly. With a glance, Augusto ordered Jole to return to her place. Although a blurred crescent moon emerged from the blanket of fog and cast a weak glow over the world, the inside of the forest was pitch black, and Augusto was advancing from memory rather than checking where he was putting his feet. Then again, he knew this trail like the back of his hand, he had been the first to open it up, and he had kept it open over the last few years, partly because he had knocked down a few trees and regularly cleared bushes and brambles, although every summer they reconquered space and ground.

They were continually accompanied by disturbing noises and the cries of animals, almost as if they were being welcomed to a kingdom barred to human beings.

As she walked, Jole shivered a little, thinking how different the woods were by day and by night. *By night all woods are the same*, she told herself, *and all are frightening*. She thought of the forest of broad-leaved trees she was going through, a forest she knew well but which seemed an unknown quantity to her in the dead of night. She recalled the hues of early autumn that had changed the colour of the woods in the last few days, the reds and yellows and ochres that, if it had been day, would have shone on maples, chestnuts, beeches, birches, oaks, alders and hornbeams. And she imagined the thousand scents those trees would have given off and the constant, infinite play of light that the sun would have set in motion as it filtered through their branches.

But here and now, everything was dark, darker than a deep silence.

God knows if the sunlight filtering through the branches has a name, Jole thought, listening to the rhythmic sound of her own boots. *God knows what it's called in the big cities.*

Augusto came to an abrupt halt.

They both stood there motionless, Augusto even holding his breath as he looked around. At that moment, a weak ray of moonlight percolated through the mist and lit up his face and Jole was able to make out his attentive, vigilant, alert look, like the look of a roebuck that has sensed a dangerous presence. She concentrated on certain details of her father's tense face, which seemed carved out of porphyry. It was barely visible, and yet in it, in the abrupt, cautious movements of his eyes, Jole glimpsed something mysterious, something bestial, which she found hard to understand, something that had taken shape with the passing of the minutes and the progress of their steps. She was even more moved.

After a few moments, without saying anything, Augusto resumed the downhill path, and she immediately followed him, surrounded by these disturbing noises, these animal cries coming from every direction—screeching, howling, whistling, breathing and whimpering—which scared Hector, too, and actually slowed him down.

15

DURING THE DESCENT, Jole slipped several times and on a couple of occasions actually ended up on her backside. She got up again immediately, without her father's help. Just over an hour after leaving home, the two De Boers, through provident changes of direction and sudden shortcuts, got to within no more than a hundred paces of the Brenta. Remaining well hidden amid the hazels, they stopped to catch their breath and listen to the water running smoothly and continuously over the rocks and stones that lay strewn on the riverbed, having been carried down by the flood three years earlier. In the meantime, the mist had started to clear, giving way to an ever clearer sky in which, apart from the moon, they even began to make out a handful of stars. Beyond the river, on the side opposite to where father and daughter now stood, they could make out the imposing wall of forest that rose all the way up to the slopes of Mount Grappa.

Augusto observed the river, then examined the sky and finally looked at his daughter.

"It was better when it was foggy," he said in a low voice, "although there aren't usually any customs men here." Then he raised his right arm and pointed at something only he could see. "We have to ford the river at that point to get to the right bank. We'll cross the valley, climb back up the mountain opposite and then go north-east, towards the border."

She nodded, and then immediately thought again of these words: in fifteen years she had never heard her father say so many together, one after the other.

Augusto moved slowly, holding the mule's reins tightly in his right hand, and Jole stuck close to the animal. Remaining deep in the brush, they descended for another thirty metres or so and at last came to the dry, stony bank of the river. Without wasting any time, they headed straight for the water. Even though the noise was growing ever louder, they could hear the distant clangour from Tezze, upriver, where the Austro-Hungarians were finishing the railway that came down from Trento, made its way through the Sugana Valley and ended up on the border with the Kingdom of Italy a few kilometres further north. For a year now, work had been continuing day and night, thousands of soldiers of the emperor and workers coming and going between the river and the nearby stone quarries, in lines and in groups, as orderly as tireless ants, equipped with pickaxes and shovels and handcarts loaded with dynamite.

To the north, towards Trento, teams of workers were digging and opening up tunnels beneath the mountains of the Sugana Valley, and further down other teams of workers were blowing up the quarries to extract the stones that they then would chisel down to size in order to lay them where other men would place sleepers of wood from Carinthia or the Fiemme Valley. Other workers were heating iron in kilns set

47

up in open country and passing it on to teams who specialized in placing and fixing the rails. Controllers travelled about in handcars, checking the quality of the work, and everywhere there were iron bridges and subways and supporting walls built with cement from Kufstein. All this endless, colossal work in order to build the tracks on which one day a steam locomotive as black and shiny as an oil spill would run. And all this technical novelty, all this devilry, came from other countries, God alone knew how distant.

Jole did not even know what a train was, nor was Augusto able to imagine one, even though one summer afternoon he had looked down from a height and seen a large number of soldiers busy laying these strange iron rails that followed the course of the Brenta.

He had heard talk of them. There were those who said that the coming of the railways would eliminate borders and bring well-being, wealth and progress to everyone, but Augusto De Boer was not at all convinced. The way he saw it, the poor would remain poor for ever and borders, all kinds of borders, would never cease to exist. At most, they might continue to move a bit this way and a bit that way, as they had done ever since man had come into existence on the face of the earth.

He and his daughter, though, saw nothing of all this turmoil, and they wisely kept their distance as they approached the river, at least three kilometres south of the borderline.

16

THEY ENTERED THE RIVER where the level of the water was significantly lower, close to a small natural weir of heaped rocks. Hector planted his forelegs and bent his head to drink, and father and daughter seized the opportunity, too: they took their respective canteens from their rucksacks and drank a little, then refilled them. After a few minutes they set off again, slowly, crossing the Brenta just below the natural weir, taking care to place their feet on the largest stones sticking up out of the water, stones polished smooth by the current. Augusto's steps were sure and firm, but Jole's were not: she kept losing her balance and ending up with her boots in the icy water.

Having reached the opposite bank, father and daughter looked around and without delay headed for the mountain, quickly entering the woods, giving the towns and villages a wide berth.

"Good!" Augusto said, beginning to climb the slope. He knew that, although the journey they had ahead of them would be long and tiring and the dangers countless, the fact that they had come down from Nevada and crossed the river unscathed was nevertheless positive and encouraging. So far, everything had gone well, apart from Jole's soaked boots, which hardly counted.

They advanced slowly, one behind the other: Augusto, Hector, Jole. Every now and then, father and daughter would stop to catch their breath, but these were just pauses of a few seconds and they would leave again immediately. The ascent was hard, and the woods so thick and rugged that apart from the effort of climbing they also had to take into account the difficulties of making their way between shrubs, branches, tangled undergrowth and brambles. They had now been travelling for two and a half hours, and they were halfway up.

Jole began to stop every hundred paces, then every fifty, then every twenty. At a certain point, she stopped and did not move. Her father turned and saw that she was in difficulty. They remained silent for a few seconds, both panting.

"Later, we'll be at altitude most of the time," he said softly, without moving his mouth or moustache, "at least until Mount Pavione and the border. Then we'll have to do some more climbing."

She nodded, indicating that she was ready to leave again. They resumed their ascent, and she tried to ignore the exhaustion eating away at their ankles and thighs and calves, concentrating instead on the importance of their objective and the need that had driven them to undertake this journey.

She thought about the gentleness and kindness her mother had always shown her and about her sister's full, cheerful laughter, even when they had to suffer hunger and the injustices inflicted by the customs officers and the Tobacco Company. She thought about her brother, so intelligent and bright even though he was born up there, in a mountain place forgotten by all the saints in heaven. Last but not least, she thought about her father, and she watched him over the back of the mule as he walked ahead of her, advancing resolutely, fearlessly, towards a goal that meant the hope of a better life for his wife and children but was also a personal, irresistible call to freedom.

She saw him as a rock, the pillar of her world. She could not imagine a future for her and her family without him, just as it is impossible to imagine the world without the sun. As she panted with the effort of the climb, her father's strong smell reached her: his skin, his sweat. For a moment, she was overcome with emotion. She no longer recognized her father, but glimpsed in him a kind of ancestral spirit. At that instant, he seemed to her a kind of *mazariòl*, a spirit of the woods, a shaman, a being more wild than civilized, a wolf. As they climbed, she saw and recognized the lone wolf that dwelt in her father's soul.

In the dead of night and in the middle of this dark, tangled, dangerous forest, it seemed to her that her father had been transformed. She had never seen him like this: in every way like a wild beast. She felt her breath go from her. Then he came close to her and stroked her head and gestured to her that everything was all right. And Jole realized that she had never loved anyone as she loved her father.

When they stopped, three and a half hours had passed since their departure. The air was cold and biting, but they were as hot and sweaty as if it were a summer's day. They drank and peered through the branches of a spruce at the Brenta Valley below them. They could see that they were already at quite a height, and Augusto knew they had almost reached the promontory. "We'll soon get to fresh water," he said.

There was no longer any trace of mist, and in the sky millions of stars glittered. The cries of the nocturnal animals were repeated and insistent, constant warnings of the presence of unknown human figures. Often, Augusto would stop for a few moments and prick up his ears and sniff the surrounding area, to hear or scent possible dangers, presences. Not of wild beasts, but of customs men.

He did not fear wild beasts at all. He did not fear bears or lynxes or wolves. He did not love them and he did not hate them.

He felt they were his brothers in a common destiny.

"Five hundred paces and we're there," he said in a low voice, looking furtively around the area.

They exchanged glances. Jole let her hair down and then tied it again, also rearranging the red kerchief her mother had tied around her neck.

"Everything all right?" he asked.

"Yes."

She looked down from the crag and saw the river, silvery in the moonlight.

She could not believe that just a little while earlier she had crossed that river. And if it had not been for her boots, which were still a little wet, she would have thought it had been a dream. She continued to stare at the Brenta, as if spellbound. She had never seen it from this bank, from the side opposite where her native village was. It struck her that she had never before been so far from home. It seemed to her that she had been away for days, when in fact not even four hours had passed.

"We have to get up there before dawn," Augusto said.

Jole took a deep breath, put her right hand on Hector's back and said, "Go!"

They set off again and before long became aware of the sound of a stream and the rumble of a little waterfall. They walked some more and finally came to within a short distance of a pool of green water, a couple of metres deep, into which the stream flowed.

Hector breathed through his nostrils and pulled with all the strength he had in order to reach the stream and bury his muzzle in the water.

Father and daughter filled their canteens again.

17

THEY REACHED THE TOP of the promontory in the first light of dawn and settled in a little hollow hidden and sheltered from the wind and from sight.

Augusto hobbled Hector to the trunk of a chestnut tree and Jole lay down beneath an *aier*, the Alpine maple so common in these parts. She looked up at the clear, rosy sky. Her legs were worn out and her eyes were closing with sleep.

From the grass around her emerged the vaporous breath of the nocturnal damp, warmed by the first rays of the sun. Thrushes, chaffinches, serins and bullfinches were singing at full tilt and bustling from branch to branch of the trees.

Augusto took his rifle with him and reconnoitred the surrounding area. He noted animals tracks and waste matter in the grass, which was still quite thick around them.

In the last few days, he observed, stags, roes, wild sheep, foxes and wolves had passed this way, but fortunately no human being. On his way back to the hollow where they had stopped to rest, Augusto found porcini mushrooms.

Rejoining his daughter, he put down the rifle, sat down next to her and took from his rucksack a knife, a little old bread and some *sopressa* salami. He cut a little of the salami, sliced a mushroom and stuck it all together inside the hunk of bread.

"Here!" he said to his daughter, holding it out to her.

She sat up and gladly took it. "What about you?" she asked him.

"First the holy water," he said, lifting the half-litre bottle of grappa to his mouth. "In an hour, we'll go," he added, once he had taken a swig, and immediately put some tobacco in his mouth. "We'll get to the border tomorrow night. It'll be hard, so for now rest a little."

How many times had he talked to her before? Jole wondered. She felt suddenly happy, but also scared. Her father was vigilant, mistrustful. The customs men could be anywhere. After a few moments, she felt reassured. With him, nothing could happen.

Having finished the last mouthful, she let down her hair and lay down again on her back.

The morning wind gently moved the branches of the trees above her, and between the patches of sky opening and closing beyond the branches she caught sight of a pair of sparrowhawks circling slowly in search of prey.

From a pocket, she took the little wooden horse—her good-luck charm—and laid it on her chest, between her breasts.

She felt her eyelids getting ever heavier. An ant crawled over her neck, making her itch, and she flicked it away with a finger.

Then she fell asleep.

PART TWO

1

W HEN SHE WOKE, the first thing she saw was the branches above her, the foliage of the trees swaying between the earth and the sky. The branches were bigger than the last time, as were the trunks of the trees that supported them: ashes, alders and oaks partly stripped by the Alpine autumn.

Without getting up, she raised her head and back and propped herself on her elbows and forearms. The little wooden horse fell from her chest, darker and more worn than before.

Three years had passed. Three years since she had fallen asleep in this very spot. Three years since she had been here the first time, with her father. Three long years since she had become a smuggler. In all that time, many things had happened and many other things had never happened again.

Since that first journey of hers in 1893, Jole had learnt a great deal about tobacco smuggling. Just as she had learnt a great deal about how to barter tobacco for metals and metals for food. That time, three years earlier, she and her father had managed to earn a pig, three sacks of flour, six capons and a few lire, spent by Augusto on potatoes, corn and chard. Returning to Nevada from that first expedition, she had felt like a real woman. That day, she was sure she had for ever thrown overboard all her fears, the insecurities of her soul and

59

her youth. She had felt suddenly grown-up, even though she was barely fifteen.

Now she was eighteen and her father was no longer here.

She lay still, looking up through the branches at a deep-blue sky, just like the sky that day. She closed her eyes and breathed in as much air as possible through her nose.

She gathered two pine cones from the ground and played with them, holding them in one hand.

It was 29th October 1896.

She thought about the last time she had seen her father. How could she have imagined then that she would never again be able to clasp him in her arms?

He had left at the age of forty-two and everyone had waved goodbye to him just as in September we wave goodbye to summer, knowing perfectly well that after autumn, winter and spring it will return in all its splendour and warm our skin and our hearts. But that had not happened.

His wife and children had waited for him in vain for days and weeks, but he had not returned.

Agnese had prayed day and night, hoping that her husband had merely been the victim of an unforeseen setback. She was sure he would reappear sooner or later. None of them left to go and look for him: that would have been pointless. On the one hand, they were waiting for him to come back by himself, counting on his strength and on the power of fate and their prayers; on the other, they could not abandon the fields, because in his absence, if they wanted to eat, they needed to toil twice as hard as before.

Then the first snow had arrived and the mountains had been buried under a white blanket metres deep. The paths had become impassable, putting paid to any idea of going to look for him. And together with the grass of the meadows and the bushes on the edges of the woods, their hope of seeing him again was also buried. Above all, of seeing him alive.

One day the following spring, a shepherd passing through Nevada had told Agnese, who had aged in a short time, that just under a year earlier he had heard about a man resembling Augusto De Boer. According to what he had been told, the man had been killed by Austrian border guards. Nevertheless, Agnese had never lost the insane hope of embracing her man again and had continued to pray to all the saints every day that God granted the earth.

Of all this Jole was thinking again, three years later, in the middle of her journey as a solitary smuggler, lying amid the autumn colours, hidden in this wood overlooking the Brenta Valley from the side opposite Nevada. Her sister and brother, who were now thirteen and ten, would have liked to come with her, just as she had done with their father, but Jole was steadfast and unmovable: she would go alone.

Either alone or she would not go.

And since she knew the way and had already risked her life three years earlier, they had yielded in the end and let her go. She needed to do it because they were hungry. There had been famine that spring, and things had been really bad for the De Boers. The family had managed to hide several dozen kilos of tobacco from the king's customs men and Jole had persuaded her mother to let her go. Agnese had lost a husband and had no desire to lose one of her daughters, too, but faced with Jole's stubbornness and the pangs of hunger in her own stomach she had come around to the idea. And so Jole had prepared herself to leave alone, in her father's footsteps, to do what he had taught her to do, what he had left her as an inheritance.

Still half lying, looking up at the sky, she thought again about her departure, the preparations, the emotion she had felt. She looked at her horse Samson, three-quarters a Haflinger. The animal was forced to move his muscles constantly to repel the horseflies tormenting him. He was bigger, stronger and more beautiful than Hector, and he would be perfect for this journey.

He was a workhorse, small and rather squat, and had been entrusted to her a year and a half earlier by the foreman of the marble quarry where she always went to admire these animals. He had injured one of his forelegs and was of no more use at the quarry.

"We have to send him to the slaughterhouse," the foreman had told Jole.

She had tenderly approached the horse. "Give him to me, I'll take care of him."

"Oh, yes, of course you will!"

"When he's recovered, I'll bring him back to you."

The foreman had thought it over for a moment and then, moved by compassion for this girl who had come there every week since she was a child out of a love of horses, had exclaimed, "Take him away, if you can get him to move. Do it before I change my mind!"

Slowly she had returned home with the horse and had made a place for him in the shed. He was beautiful: hazelnut and chestnut, with a blond mane and tail, just like Jole's hair. Fascinated by that mane, she had christened him Samson.

She had treated him every day with compresses and medicinal ointments made from wild herbs and resin, and within a few months he had completely recovered and had even begun to gallop again, a little at a time.

The preparations for departure had been anything but hasty or rushed. Her father had taught her to consider every single detail of the journey, to avoid the risk of getting into situations that could have been avoided with a little foresight. And so Jole had prepared everything with care and attention during the week preceding her departure, leaving nothing to chance.

She had collected just the right quantity of tobacco from the various hiding places, weighed it, obtained water, fitted and filled all the bags and cases in which the tobacco was to be hidden during the journey, let the horse rest and feed more than usual, wrapped pieces of Morlacco and Bastardo cheese and *sopressa* salami in thick sheets of paper, put dried beans and potatoes in small jute sacks, checked her boots, and dug out two large blankets, two rucksacks, a few ropes, a large steel canteen, a rough hemp sheet and a lantern. She had hidden the eighty kilos of tobacco—in leaf, powder and shag form—partly among the things she had loaded on Samson's flanks and partly in her own clothes. Last but not least, she had gone to the shed, opened an old oakwood chest and taken out St Paul, the Werndl-Holub rifle that had lost its brother.

She had learnt to shoot during the year of her first journey. It had been her father who had taught her to fire with his rifle, that St Peter he always carried with him on his smuggling expeditions and which had disappeared along with him and his mule.

2

Now, in this wood that was the first halt on her new journey, thinking again about the past but above all about the future that awaited her, she got to her feet and stooped to pick up her little wooden horse, which had fallen on the infinite cloak of leaves that carpeted the undergrowth. She tied her hair, which in the last three years had become much longer, tied her old red kerchief around her neck and put on the broad-brimmed straw hat that had been her father's. Last but not least, she grabbed the rifle and put it over her shoulder, just as a gust of wind sent dozens of leaves swirling through the air.

At that moment, Jole heard the loud whistle of the steam locomotive coming from the Sugana Valley, perhaps from Grigno, much further down. The railway had been inaugurated a few months earlier and had already begun to clatter back and forth from the border down to the valley.

With her hat tilted forward and the rifle over her shoulder pressed against her rucksack, she went to Samson, stroked his muzzle and mounted him in one confident, accurate bound. On her Haflinger, she was more beautiful than ever, and it seemed as if nothing could ever stop her.

"Ya!" she said softly, and at this command Samson set off again.

Even though she had a clear memory of the route she had taken with her father, she knew that her journey would not be at all easy, since every step would hide a thousand pitfalls.

"Ya!" she repeated.

And, riding bareback, she left the smell of sad memories in that place, along with her own smell: Jole, the young smuggler.

3

S HE ENTERED THE WOOD very slowly, constantly looking around, alert to any possible threatening presences. She knew that at any moment she might encounter Italian customs men, wild animals or criminals ready to do anything to prey on wayfarers and smugglers.

She wondered which of these three misfortunes might have befallen her father but could not answer her own question, since she considered him cleverer than any customs officer, stronger than any natural adversary and more ruthless than any brigand who might be encountered in the forests.

The sun had been up for a couple of hours and was now starting to lick the ridge of Mount Grappa, spilling its golden rays over the north side of that sacred mountain.

She veered east and then north-east like a fugitive, never leaving the thickest part of the wood, concealed by the vegetation, camouflaged like a viper lying in the undergrowth.

She almost never stopped, except to check possible signs of other people having passed that way or to get a better sense of direction, choosing routes impossible to spot or discover from any other position. Leaving the northern slope of Mount Grappa behind her, she saw the valley of the Cismon ahead, and at this point, in order to continue the journey, she had to make up her mind to leave the dense wood of black horn-beams, mountain maples and lindens and cross first a birch forest and then some meadows and pastures that stretched for several kilometres in the direction she would have to follow. This was a delicate moment, because, although Jole had skil-fully positioned herself more than five hundred metres above the village of Arsiè, there was a real risk that someone might see her from there. Before coming out into the open, she dismounted and tied her horse to the base of the trunk of a thick birch. She reconnoitred the area for a radius of about a hundred metres then went back to Samson, who was almost impossible to make out among these dappled trees.

Everything was fine, and she felt ready to continue, but first she walked her horse to the edge of the wood, where the birches thinned out and gave way to the autumn meadows. There she let him graze for almost an hour, during which she stretched her legs and gathered some chanterelles and parasol mushrooms sticking up from a patch of moss a few paces from her. She cleaned them with the knife she had in her belt and put them in one of the leather bags tied around the horse's flanks.

After a while she thought she saw something move, not so far away, in the meadow, something like a large shapeless black patch that had appeared suddenly and immediately vanished behind a grassy rise. Alarmed, she took out her rifle in two rapid moves. Then she lay down on the ground and aimed at the rise, waiting to get an idea of what it had been.

Holding the barrel straight, head and shoulders still in a firing position, she felt her heart pounding. Her anxious breathing might make it hard for her to aim. She lay there motionless for a few seconds, her rifle still trained on the spot where she had glimpsed that black, indistinct thing moving. Seconds that seemed like minutes, minutes that seemed like hours.

All at once, that big dark shadow came out into the open, making a terrible racket. Heaving a sigh of relief, Jole lowered St Paul. It was only a big wood grouse, which promptly raised its tail feathers and began emitting shrill, threatening cries.

Without hesitating for too long, since she knew that some specimens could be aggressive, Jole went back to Samson, untied him and immediately resumed her journey, leaving the woods and the grouse behind her and at last reaching the open spaces that would lead her to her goal.

For a few hours, she climbed a long pastureland plateau made up of green hills carpeted with millions of purple autumn crocuses. The sky was clear and the sun beat down on Jole's neck and on the coat of her horse, who went on, metre after metre, without ever complaining, even though his body was lathered in sweat.

4

S HE LEFT FONZASO behind her, remaining constantly at
altitude and always alert to the possible presence of customs
officers or royal soldiers. In these meadows she came across
hares, francolins, partridges and young roe deer in the company
of their mothers, and none of them seemed frightened by her
passing. She actually had the impression they were somehow
welcoming her to this place. Under the strong midday sun,
the autumn colours were bright and bold and she could not
help admiring them, forgetting for a moment what she was
doing and the reason she was here for the second time in her
life. But then she remembered the time she had passed this
way with her father.

Their journey had taken place at the end of September,
and the autumn had not yet been so ablaze with colour. She
recalled the words he had said to her when they had come
through here: "You see those over there? They're the Vette
Feltrine."

Jole had followed the direction of his gaze until her eyes
came to rest on those peaks.

After a few moments he had resumed speaking. "Jole, this
journey has only one rule: not to come back as you left. Return
home different!"

"And how do you do that?"

"A professional smuggler is like the wind. He mustn't show himself, mustn't let himself be caught and must always be ready to change direction."

Jole had smiled, and her father had put a handful of tobacco in his mouth and started to chew it slowly.

Samson was proceeding at a steady pace, rocking her gently to right and left. Jole slightly lifted the brim of her hat, almost completely uncovering her forehead. She looked at the grey, rocky peaks emerging between the hills in front of her and recognized them.

I have to reach them by tomorrow morning, she thought, *then climb almost to the top of Mount Pavione, where the border with Austria is, and go down again on the other side, beyond the border.*

Her lips and mouth and throat felt dry. Samson was thirsty, too, and as time passed his tongue had become very large and thick. Without thinking, Jole grabbed the canteen from the horse's flank and raised it to her mouth. Unfortunately, it was no longer so fresh: they needed to find a stream. After another half hour, instead of slowing down with fatigue and thirst, Samson began gradually to increase his pace and to quiver, almost to tremble, as if something, some brute force, was urging him to keep going forward. Jole realized that he had scented water, and she went along with him until he started to move ever more rapidly and before long reached a trickle of water that ran down a slope and soon turned into a small stream.

Jole dismounted and filled her canteens further upstream. Samson drank his fill and then together they withdrew behind a little wood a short distance away. They rested a little and Jole ate some salami and Morlacco with black bread, then thought seriously about resuming her journey.

Just then, she heard voices coming from the wood.

Listening more intently, she recognized them as Italian voices.

She stroked Samson's muzzle. "Quiet now," she said, and the horse relaxed.

She tied him to a tree and took a few steps in the direction of the voices, careful to remain under cover. At first she just about made out the sound, but then other details gradually came into focus. They were men, four of them, perhaps five, and they were laughing and joking. She hid behind an oak at the edge of the wood and tried to identify them.

After a few moments, she knew who they were: customs officers.

Her hands felt sweaty and her heart was in her mouth. She watched them for a moment, her hand tight on the little wooden horse she kept in one of her pockets. Then she saw that, luckily, they were heading towards the opposite side from where she was and were descending towards Fonzaso.

Gradually, their voices grew fainter until they disappeared down the mountainside. Jole watched them until they were just tiny dots. Then they disappeared completely.

She heaved a sigh of relief and went back to Samson.

"Let's go," she said. "Everything's fine."

She continued for a few more hours. The rocky mountains, which were the same colour as her eyes, grew larger as she advanced towards their slopes.

She came to a deep blue lake set in a wild basin, its shores populated with choughs and wagtails. Buzzards circled endlessly in the sky, repeatedly emitting their hunting cries.

She advanced some more until she came to another stream that plunged into a raging waterfall. She stopped and listened with eyes closed to the wonderful roar of its waves, and a fine dusting of icy water rose from the current and washed her wind- and sun-reddened face, offering her welcome relief from the heat.

Some fifty paces from her, on the same bank, she saw a large hare. Now was the right time and place to fire, she thought. With the clamour of the waterfall, nobody would be able to hear the shot.

She took the rifle, aimed at the hare and with one shot blew it away. She dismounted to collect it and smiled when she saw how big it was. She tied it proudly to one of the laces hanging from Samson's harness and went on her way.

Just before sunset, hungry and exhausted, she came to a place that her father had called Val Storta: an Alpine basin which descended rapidly from a cleft in the rocks to a meadow flanked by two high cliffs that sheltered it from the biting winds. There Jole came across a cowherd with his Burlina cows: she counted twenty-seven in his herd.

The sky was bright blue, and the only two clouds that stood out were suffused with the yellow and pink and gold of sunset. The air had quickly turned light, brisk and prickly.

She rode slowly through the cows towards the cowherd, who watched her coming impassively, his eyes full of yearning, the way all cowherds look when they return from the summer pasture after being isolated from the world for months on end.

She remembered what was said in Nevada about the cowherds, which was that they were always staring into space because during those weeks of solitude the witches and *anguine*—the spirits of the woods—had stolen their memories and sometimes even their souls.

Remaining on her horse, she drew level with him and greeted him.

In response, he raised one arm.

Jole looked around, pushed her hat back on her brow and introduced herself. "My name is Vich," she said, lying about her surname. "Jole Vich."

"Toni Zonch. How do you do?"

His face was dirty and burnt by the sky, his hands seemed like the tangled branches of a locust tree and his clothes stank of wind and rain and urine.

She dismounted and they spoke a little. Toni was only sixteen, although he looked twenty years older. He lived near Arsiè and in a few days' time would be returning to his village after pasturing his cows on the Vette Feltrine.

"There's a cowshed up there, half an hour's walk from here," he said, "and that's where I lived in the summer. After a season at altitude, going back home seems the easiest thing, but actually it's the hardest, because that's when wolves and bears attack the herd."

"Does that happen?"

"Two days ago I lost two young calves near here, torn to pieces by wolves."

"Don't you have a rifle?"

"Yes, I do, but in some cases it's not much use."

"It's not much use if you don't know how to use it," she said. "Shall we share our dinner?" she added, seizing the hare by the ears and showing it to him.

They camped out, she with her rifle loaded and he with his three mangy dogs, who seemed even more distracted than their master. They lit a fire behind a crag so as not to be seen, skinned the hare and roasted it on a spit, then Jole took out some old bread and Toni offered her Burlina cow's milk and smoked roebuck meat. They spent the rest of the time in silence more than in speech, watching the tongues of fire as it crackled at the foot of the crag, the sparks rising into the dark sky.

She thought again about her journey and the effort it had involved.

Her legs were hard and painful, her back felt as if it was broken and her arse bruised and numb from bouncing on Samson's withers.

"Why aren't you going back to the cowshed tonight?" she asked.

"Because it would be more risky going back up there than staying here. I'm behind, because I lost a cow and spent hours searching for it. By the time I stopped, the sun was already starting to set. I wouldn't have had time to get back to the shed. It's better to stay here tonight."

"I can see that."

"But you're a smuggler, aren't you?"

"No."

He smiled. "I've told you what I do, where I come from and where I'm going, and you haven't told me a damned thing."

She said nothing.

"Have it your way, it makes no difference. You can trust me anyway. I wouldn't gain anything by denouncing you to the police. That lot are bigger criminals than the criminals."

Jole burst out laughing, then stood up and went over to Samson. When she came back to the fire, she offered the cowherd a small handful of shag and a dry birch leaf.

He rolled the curls of tobacco in the leaf, licked it and finally lit it. His eyes closed, he voluptuously breathed in the dense, strong-smelling blue smoke.

"You've given me a wonderful gift," he said after two deep drags.

"For your hospitality."

"For that you must thank the stars."

"I already have."

"So, you're carrying tobacco. I knew it. I've never seen a woman smuggler before."

"Here I am!"

"Who are you thinking of giving the tobacco to around here? The chamois and the mouflons?"

"I'm going across the border."

He opened wide his eyes, which for a moment seemed to have come back to life, then said, "Oh, the Krauts. I don't

76

want to know anything more, but it's going to be hard, you know that?"

"This isn't the first time I've done it."

Continuing to savour the cigarette, the cowherd lay down on the ground, his eyes turned to the sky.

In the meantime, the air had grown cold, and around the two of them there was nothing to be seen. In spite of the crackling of the fire, they could clearly hear the howling of wolves.

"Do you hear them?" the cowherd asked.

She clutched St Paul to her and said, "They won't come tonight."

She was far from sure of that, of course, but out of personal pride she did not want to appear insecure. Spending the night with someone else was better than spending it alone, but she knew it was good not to trust anyone.

Out of the blue, she said, "Have you ever met a man named Augusto De Boer?"

"At pasture you meet lots of wild animals, but no humans."

"Not very tall, black moustache."

"No. Where would I have met him?"

"Here or anywhere, in the last two years."

"What did this man do to you?"

She did not reply.

They were silent for a few minutes more, looking at the fire, then Jole discreetly moved away.

"Night," she said to him.

"Night!"

They each prepared for sleep, fifty paces from one another.

Jole lay down next to Samson, covered herself with two coarse woollen blankets and looked up at the sky above her.

There were a large number of stars, big shiny stars sparkling like multicoloured fountains of life. It seemed to her as if they had a voice and were about to tell her something. They wanted to say benign words to her, she thought, words of good omen. Then she realized the stupidity of that romantic idea. If her father had heard her, he would have made fun of her.

5

THOSE THREE YEARS without Augusto had been very difficult for the De Boers. Keeping the house, the cowshed and, above all, the *masiere* going had proved harder than they might have imagined. Growing Nostrano tobacco was a task as delicate as it was laborious, and only the head of the family knew all its secrets, from the planting to the drying. Agnese and Jole had divided up the tasks that had always been Augusto's, but because of their inexperience things had not always gone well.

God, if you exist, bring my father home soon, Jole had thought one day in June as she was washing the shoots of tobacco.

Agnese, a few metres away, had thought the same thing, and as she worked with stooped back, her long hair peeking out from the kerchief, she had moved her lips to pray to that God in whom she had a blind faith, that same God whom Jole had never known in her life.

6

T HE NEXT DAY she woke late. When she opened her eyes the sun was already high and the air mild. She sat up abruptly and saw that Samson was beside her as if to protect her.

She realized that she had slept more than she should, which was bound to affect her timetable. She got to her feet and folded the blankets. She looked around and noticed that there was nobody there, neither the Burlina cows nor their young cowherd, who must have gone back to the cowshed to milk them. She checked to see if everything was in its place: her equipment, the food, the tobacco.

It was all there. She took fifty paces and noticed that a thin thread of smoke was still rising from the fire that she and the cowherd had lit the evening before. That was not to her liking: someone might have been able to see it, even from a distance. She kicked the embers and ashes and extinguished the last remaining lighted coals.

She quickly washed her face in a little stream that ran beneath one of the two cliffs and then, seeing that the sun had warmed the air a little, decided she would also take off the jerseys she was wearing and wash her neck and breasts. On contact with the cold water she shivered and goose pimples appeared on her skin. She dried herself with a cloth, quickly dressed, filled the canteens and set off again in a northerly direction, towards Mount Pavione, leaving those open, limitless spaces and going back into the forests of broad-leaved trees that would conceal her presence until early afternoon.

She and her horse advanced between hazels and locust trees, downy oaks, black hornbeams, beeches, maples, ashes and chestnut trees. Jole proceeded without stopping once, cautious and furtive, but also sure that she was quite protected from the customs patrols and convinced that she would make up for the time she had lost. After a while, the mountainside began to grow ever steeper. The climb ahead of her was going to be a hard one.

After hours of travelling, Samson was tired again, and Jole decided to stop and get a better idea of where she was. She tied the horse to the trunk of an ash and proceeded on foot for a while, climbing back up the ridge to see if there were any gaps in the vegetation that would her help find her bearings.

At last she came to a small promontory from which the massif of Mount Pavione could clearly be made out, its slopes now less than two hours' journey away, although all of it uphill.

She ran down to get Samson, sliding and tumbling a couple of times in the undergrowth, which was covered in dry leaves.

"Keep going!" she said to the horse, stroking his blond mane. "Another couple of hours and then we'll stop until tomorrow morning."

For a while she continued on foot, holding Samson by the reins to make it easier for him, although it was certainly not his mistress's weight that bothered him, but rather the wearying length of the journey and the load he was carrying.

The ascent grew uneven. As they proceeded, the woods around them changed colour and smell. They left behind them the broad-leaved trees and entered a forest of spruces populated with woodpeckers, jays and squirrels.

Every now and again, the shrill, repeated call of a crow would announce their presence to all the animals of the forest.

Every now and again, Samson would drink at a puddle or a trickle of water emerging from the undergrowth.

Every now and again, Jole would wonder if she was ever going to make it.

After a while they came to a clearing, and from there Jole was able to make out the Croce d'Aune pass, a long way below them.

She drank from the canteen, feeling cheered because it seemed to her that she had passed this way with her father. Without lingering, she went back into the woods and continued on foot beneath the Vette Feltrine, towards the great Mount Pavione, which rose majestically ahead of her.

After half an hour, exhausted, she stopped for a moment to get a better look at it.

There was something totemic, almost sacred about it.

That's it, that's the mountain! That's the border!

Just beyond its ridge was the border with Austria, with the Tyrol, and on the side opposite that wall were the Noana Valley and the Primiero Valley, where she was headed.

It was four in the afternoon when she got back on Samson, and for another half hour she rode on, constantly climbing.

When the sun again slipped behind the mountains, Jole decided that the moment had come to stop, but she wanted to make sure of finding the ideal spot, a safe place. A few minutes later, she heard strange noises coming from her left and froze like a statue. She took the rifle, slowly dismounted and slipped between the branches of the spruce trees and their highly intricate roots coming up from the ground.

She was curious to find out what it was.

She saw that the forest opened onto a small area of beaten earth. It was from there that the noises were coming: what seemed like the sounds of breaking branches and sharp blows. She leant forward a little more and clearly saw a man in the process of building a large woodpile.

He had only just started, but had already planted three wooden poles in the ground, held together by two rings formed from branches. The man stopped for a moment, took a bottle from a large bag and drank greedily. At that moment, Jole accidentally trod on a dry branch and snapped it.

The noise alerted the man, who turned towards the woods where Jole was hiding.

"Who goes there?" he cried, brandishing a shovel.

Now that she had been discovered, it was pointless to hide: the man would come and look for her. She decided to come out into the open.

She put her rifle over her shoulder to show that she was not a threat, took two steps and emerged from the woods.

"It's me!" she cried as she did so.

"And who might you be?"

"I'm just passing through. I heard noises and wanted to see what it was."

"Haven't you ever seen a charcoal burner at work?" he said, raising the bottle to his lips again.

Jole took a few steps forward and looked at him more closely. He had a huge stomach, a swollen, ruddy face and large, good-natured eyes. "No."

They shook hands.

"Jole!"

"Guglielmo."

She noticed that he stank of grappa.

"And where are you from, Jole?"

"The Brenta Valley, more or less."

"Tobacco?"

"No."

He laughed. "Then what's that rifle for, girl? You haven't come here to kill me, by any chance?"

"Maybe, who knows?"

They both laughed. Then he drank some more grappa. "Well, sorry if I'm not the best of company," he said, wiping his mouth with his sleeve, "but as you can see I'm busy. I'm stopping here for a few days before I go back to Santa Monica with a bit of charcoal. That's what I do for a living. Santa Monica is the village where I live, down there, beyond the Val Storta. You can do whatever you like. If you want to camp around here for the night, go ahead. And now, excuse me, but I have to carry on working, these sunny days are a real blessing. It's been years since there was an Indian summer like this."

Jole smiled. "Are there customs men around here?" she asked.

The charcoal burner looked at her for a moment questioningly, then again wiped his lips with the back of his hand, looked around and said, "There's nobody, not even anyone's dog."

They both smiled.

"I'll fetch my horse and camp out here in the meadow for the night, if that's all right with you."

"Do whatever you like, girl, I have to work!"

And without looking at her, he took up his shovel again and started beating a few pieces of wood, then tied them to the branches that were holding together the three large poles stuck in the ground.

There was an all-pervading and very pleasant smell of resin and fresh timber.

She moved away from the clearing and went back into the woods to fetch Samson, who was quivering and swishing his tail constantly to swat away the multitude of insects that were molesting him, attracted by his sweat.

Then she led him back to the clearing and set up camp some distance away, beneath the stars and a crescent moon obscured by a layer of high, thin clouds that also crowned the peak of Mount Pavione. She lay down on the ground and arranged her blankets over her.

She remembered her mother, brother and sister. At the thought of them, she was moved. They felt so close and yet so far. She took out the little wooden horse she had in her pocket and clutched it to her chest.

"My darlings," she said, addressing the stars, "give me the strength to keep going and do what I have to do. I feel quite alone, but if I think of you I find the necessary strength in myself. Think of me, too. Mother, pray for me, you know how to do it."

Her moment of weakness passed. It could not be otherwise: she could not afford to give in.

Just before going to sleep, she nibbled some hardened salami and mature Bastardo and watched from a distance as the man worked ceaselessly, even after sunset, between one swig of grappa and another.

7

I T TAKES STRENGTH, guile, skill and experience to make a good charcoal pile. In a word: craft.

And Guglielmo knew how to make one, even though he was not the owner of the piles he built, he was only a labourer. His boss had men and piles in various villages on the border between the Bellunese and the Trentino, and every now and again he would make a tour of inspection to see how the work was going and pay his workers. And he had become rich on charcoal, unlike his labourers, who were always on the move from wood to wood like old ogres, trying to earn a little bread.

The charcoal was useful to everyone: in the villages, to the Austrians, to the factories making bells and cannon, and now that they were building new railways it was also needed for the locomotives.

But making a charcoal pile was not at all easy, even for Guglielmo, who had experience to spare. For some time now, the boss had been after him, and he had to do a good job.

He had cut the trees when the moon was on the wane, had divided the timber, had reduced it to lengths of about a metre, and after letting it dry for two weeks had transported it to the *jal*: the clearing where he would build the pile. The space he had chosen this time was perfect since it was away from draughts and on permeable soil. At this point, he had put the wood down in a circle, breaking the thickest timber to make it easier to burn. He had stuck three wooden poles in the ground, each two and a half metres high, holding them together with two rings formed of brushwood and small branches. It was during this phase of the work that Jole had appeared.

And even as Jole slept, the charcoal burner continued his work without wasting a minute, lighting the clearing with four torches.

He arranged the thickest wood around the three poles, then the thinner wood, in such a way as to leave the central hole free to accommodate the fire. He packed the wood as tightly as possible, closing up all cracks, and late in the night the pile at last assumed its characteristic conical shape. Then he covered it with spruce branches, topsoil and dry leaves, with the aim of insulating it.

Towards morning, just before dawn, tired but satisfied, Guglielmo lit his sacred fire.

As he moved the torch closer, his eyes seemed possessed, as if there were something magical in this gesture, as if this were a mystical and in some ways devotional ritual for which he had been preparing himself for days and at which he would have to officiate constantly for another two weeks, before cooling the pile by covering it with earth and proceeding to the stockpiling of the charcoal obtained.

With the torch in his hand, he felt like an old pagan priest. With a pole, he made two openings in the pile to create the necessary vents and then set fire to the wood in the belly of the gigantic *pojat*, as he called his creation.

8

THAT NIGHT Jole dreamt about the first time her father had let her use the rifle.

It was the spring of 1893, and she was just a few weeks from her fifteenth birthday. They had gone down through the forests and oak woods of the Brenta Valley and had stopped in a little clearing on the mountainside, a few dozen paces from the river, so that the shots would be covered by the sound of the current.

"Here!" he had said, holding out St Peter.

She had taken it with trembling hands and had realized that the rifle was cold and heavy. At such close quarters, its smell of iron and old wood was much stronger.

"Look how I hold it," Augusto had said, taking it quickly from her hands, "and do as I do."

He had shouldered St Peter, taken position, aimed at a granite rock some thirty metres away, then checked that his daughter was doing the same. Then he had given her back the weapon and gone to her to improve her posture.

"The right elbow has to be lower and the legs apart. Keep your feet solidly on the ground."

Then he had shown her how to load and immediately watched her as she did the same.

"Go on, fire at the rock!" he had said encouragingly.

Jole was tense, her hands were sweaty and the rifle seemed to weigh as much as the entire trunk of an old chestnut tree.

"Take a deep breath and fire!"

Jole breathed in, then held her breath and aimed.

She had concentrated on the violent noise of the river a few paces below them as it constantly broke on the stones sticking up from the bed. All at once it had seemed to her as if that insistent noise contained all the gunshots and all the bad noises in the world, including people's cries of pain and the desperate weeping of children. She had thought that by pressing the trigger she would put an end to that strange impression, that sinister, somewhat childish sensation. She had counted mentally to three and fired, immediately falling to the ground because of the rifle's powerful recoil.

Despite the noise of the river, the roar had echoed across the wooded slopes of Mount Grappa and the plateau.

Unperturbed, Augusto had bent over her slightly and said, "You can only fall the first time, the second you have to keep standing."

With the smell of gunpowder still lingering in the air, Jole had got to her feet and asked, "What about the rock? Did I get it, Papà?"

"The rock, no. But you almost killed me!"

9

B Y THE FIRST LIGHT OF DAWN, the charcoal pile was already lit, although it would be a few days before a steady flame from the top, like a volcano erupting, would announce the start of the carbonization process.

Getting up, Jole stared open-mouthed at that smoking volcano just a few dozen metres from her, of which there had been not even a hint the previous evening.

She looked for the charcoal burner and saw that he was busy cooking polenta on the fire. He seemed exhausted but satisfied. He looked at her and she waved to him. He replied with a smile and turned his eyes to the pile, as if to say, "Not bad, eh?"

They did not waste much time in conversing. They drank something together, and she ate a corn biscuit the man offered her. Then she resumed her journey, going back into the woods and riding Samson in the direction of Mount Pavione.

10

I T WAS A VERY HARD ASCENT, at first because the forests of black pine, spruce and silver fir surrounding the slopes were dense and tangled, and then because, when they reached the pass, the climb became all the more dangerous due to the swamps and bogs that had formed as a result of the persistent late-summer rains. Samson was having difficulty advancing, his legs sinking dangerously into that muddy earth, and Jole did not dare dismount, as it would have been impossible for her to walk in such terrain.

They advanced slowly in this way for four hours, while a flock of crows kept following them, cawing constantly, calling other birds that flew down and watched the girl and her horse struggling.

When at last the ground became hard and stony, Jole heaved a sigh of relief and the crows flew off, disappointed perhaps.

Jole and Samson proceeded with more confidence, tackling the first part of a large scree, even though the effort of the climb was starting to wear away at the horse's muscles and at that altitude the sun was beginning to scorch.

"Ya!" she cried in Samson's ear, urging him forward. To avoid tiring him too much, she undertook a zigzag route,

93

going in and out of the thickets of Swiss pine, as if following imaginary bends.

The scree on which they were was burning hot, and she hoped that all the vipers in this heap of stones were already hibernating, because if Samson were bitten, she might have to say goodbye to this adventure.

The higher she climbed, the frailer, weaker and more vulnerable she felt.

The border is just behind there, on the north side, she thought. *We're almost there. But that's why we have to watch out for soldiers.*

She knew perfectly well that because of its proximity to the border this area might be patrolled and monitored by customs officers, both Italian and Austrian. She realized that what she was confronting was certainly the most dangerous phase of the journey, as well as the most laborious.

All at once, when they were about halfway up, the sky started to cloud over rapidly. Within a very short time, it was completely overcast. Samson managed to scent a little stream that descended from the peaks and made its way between the white boulders surrounding them. So they stopped and both drank, stocking up on as much water as they could carry with them.

Jole took off her hat and drank in frantic gulps, then wiped the sweat from her forehead. She noticed that the temperature had fallen: a stiff breeze stung her temples and the skin of her neck beneath the sweat-soaked kerchief. Almost immediately, the breeze became a wind and then a squall.

It was a strange, treacherous wind, as sudden as it was unstable. As it lashed the rocks and stones and low clumps of grass, it produced a sound that resembled a battle cry, a terrible, mysterious voice from some hidden lair in the sky, a warning to whoever happened to be on that rock face.

At that moment, she remembered passing this very place with her father, and she recalled that on that occasion, too, a great wind, the same wind that was now hampering her progress, had flung itself upon them without mercy, its loud, ominous voice echoing.

"It isn't a wind like any other," her father had said with a frown.

Jole had remained silent because she knew that when the skin of her father's face creased in that way it meant that he was about to say something essential and mysterious. She had looked at him with respect and waited for him to say more, and he did.

"It isn't a wind like any other," he had repeated. "It's the legendary soul of the border, an ancient spirit at least as old as this mountain, a spirit that blows hard and moves from century to century following the borders of men."

Remembering her father's words now, Jole shuddered.

She looked up at the summit of Mount Pavione, then down at the ridge to the west, two hundred metres lower than the peaks.

"That's where we have to pass, Samson. That's our crossing place."

To regain all her strength, she thought again about her father and about her family, who were still at home, counting on her, on her strength and determination.

She remembered her departure, and her mother's eyes, as clear, bright and watery as the last ice on the April meadows.

"Mamma," she had said, mounting Samson, "I'll be back soon, you'll see."

"Be careful, Jole."

In those three years, her mother had grown as thin and dry as the branch of a larch. Antonia and little Sergio had clung to Jole's legs, on either side of the horse, as if they did not want to let her go.

"Please be careful," her sister had made sure to say, clasping her tightly.

"Of course I will, don't worry."

Sergio had given her a pinch on the thigh and made her jump.

"Ouch! What are you doing, you little devil?"

"Think of me always!"

Jole had smiled, lifted him onto the horse, ruffled his hair and given him a kiss on the brow.

She had promised them that she would make it through and would keep her word.

The wind was driving even harder now, and a gust almost blew away Jole's hat, so she folded it and put it in one of the dozens of bags Samson was carrying on his flanks together with the tobacco and everything she needed for the journey.

She looked at the sky, trying to work out what was in store for them, then at the surrounding area, her sight as sharp and attentive as that of a golden eagle. She did not see any unusual movements or any indication of the presence of customs men. In her own way, she felt lucky. She got back on Samson and said, "Not long now, my friend. From up there, we'll be able to see our goal, and if all goes well we'll be there by tonight."

They kept advancing, Jole trying to kill time and fatigue by thinking of her objective and of all the sacrifices she had had to make in eighteen years to obtain something good.

She recalled her mother's sympathetic voice, her sister's perpetually bright, kindly eyes, her little brother's daydreaming.

"Think of me always!" he had said a moment before she left.

"Now go, you stubborn De Boer!" her mother had said encouragingly. "Go before I change my mind and make you get off that horse!"

Climbing towards the summit of Mount Pavione, she took from her pocket the little wooden horse she and Sergio had carved for fun and squeezed it in her right hand as if she could get it to enter her flesh, her blood. At this difficult moment, as Samson advanced beneath her step by step, she started crying. She felt more than ever a De Boer, aware that however little she had had in her life, that little had only been thanks to the strength of her nearest and dearest.

At last, after two hours, Jole and Samson reached the crossing. They stopped at the highest point and sheltered behind a rocky spur.

Jole looked out over the north slope and pointed to a spot ahead of her.

"Look down there," she said to Samson. "The border is just beyond those pines! You can see the Noana and Primiero Valleys and the Val Canali. Mining country. Copper and silver. That's where we'll be tonight."

11

S HE STAYED THERE as little time as possible, just long
enough to drink and let Samson get a little of his strength
back. A few minutes later she began to descend, walking beside
her horse and holding tightly to the reins, given how steep and
perilous the descent was. The wind was still blowing, violent
and unceasing, and its whistling sounded like premonitory
howling, but she continued walking, planting her feet one at
a time on the crumbly terrain of the slope. Her boots beat
against the white, dusty stones of the scree, causing bruises
and blisters on her toes and putting her rudimentary footwear
to a hard test.

The descent grew ever steeper and it struck Jole that a
journey on which she only had to climb, however hard, would
have been preferable.

She cursed these sharp stones that were making her ankles
and knees and hips ache. Samson, on the other hand, was
proceeding more securely and firmly: it was not as difficult
for him as for someone who had thin human legs instead of
four powerful animal ones.

Jole stopped and looked up, even though the wind, mixed
now with dust, lashed at her eyes. She saw that the patch of
Swiss pines was now straight ahead of her and she resumed

walking. At that moment the squally wind whispered something that sounded like a harsh, threatening sentence, but when Jole and Samson at last reached the pines, it suddenly abated. The air grew still, as if paralysed beneath the rays of the sun, which now once again peeked out from behind a blanket of high, thin clouds that quickly melted away.

That disturbing voice had vanished. The soul of the border had suddenly stopped its merciless blowing.

Jole looked around. As far as she could tell, she had just crossed the border.

Further down, beyond the canyon of the Noana Valley, some of the villages in the Primiero Valley now looked bigger and more distinct. She looked behind her: the summit of Mount Pavione was high and again remote, since she had already done quite a lot of the descent. She heaved a sigh of relief and felt her hips and knees, rubbing them gently, then sat down on a round rock and took off her torn, dented boots, which were full of white and grey dust finer than cornflour.

She massaged her feet, first one then the other. They hurt a lot and she saw that there were many blisters.

Then she looked up at the surrounding mountains.

To her right, she saw for the first time the stunning beauty of the Pala range.

It held her spellbound.

She closed her eyes and said a prayer to the Madonna, more out of habit, a way of warding off bad luck, than out of genuine devotion. She loosened her hair, then tied it again and put her hat back on her head.

After a while Samson tried to attract her attention, nudging her left shoulder with his muzzle. Alerted, she tried to figure out what it was he was trying to tell her.

Just when it seemed to her that everything was calm, she spotted some men in military uniform over to her right, at the foot of the scree. She crouched and made Samson get down, too. The possibility that the Austrian customs men had seen them, or might see them, was quite remote, but it was best to keep still, not say a word, and try to work out what they were doing, hoping above all that they would soon go away. Hidden amid the low, aromatic branches of the mountain pines, Jole and Samson watched the movements of the soldiers: they might be *Zollwache*, the fearsome border guards. They had to remain in that position for nearly an hour, during which Jole took the opportunity to eat a little cheese, have a few sips of water and, above all, air her feet and treat the blisters with pine resin. She noticed that there were dandelion flowers around her, so yellow and beautiful compared with the angularity and greyness of the surrounding stones.

She picked one and looked at it carefully.

How beautiful they are! she thought, losing herself for a moment in the geometry of its petals. *This flower grows everywhere and always, on the plains and in the mountains, in every season of the year except winter, when the meadows are covered in snow. It's the true symbol of nature and freedom.*

Then she looked further, below and above her, and saw that yellow dandelion flowers were strewn all over the scree, both before and after the border, a clear sign that, unlike men, they did not recognize any borders.

All at once she saw that handful of men slowly climbing the north side of Mount Pavione.

When she was certain that they were quite high up and so much to the side of her as to make it impossible for them to see her, she put her socks and boots back on, got Samson up and resumed the descent. She had cramps in her buttocks and legs and her feet burnt like two beechwood logs thrown into the mouth of a stove.

They passed close to a group of ibex, placid and impassive, and further down saw some chamois turning frantically, dislodging stones and causing at least one genuine landslide. An hour later, at the base of the enormous scree, they came to a place called Val dei Salti, and immediately after that reached the first larches and the first conifers, widely spaced as if they did not want to make friends with each other. Then the slope became less steep for a while, before once again plunging towards the valley. Jole got back on Samson and rode into a large forest of silver firs, a forest so airy and clean as to seem a labyrinth stretching to infinity.

I've crossed the border! I've crossed the border! she kept repeating in her mind, to give herself strength.

It seemed to her that, over and above her final objective, she had already succeeded in a great enterprise.

She thought about the myth of this border, about its legends, and especially about the fact that when it comes down to it, every border is nothing but an imaginary line invented by a few men to subjugate and mistreat other men…

That was what her father had always told her, and it was what she, too, believed.

What is the meaning of borders when the trees in the woods and the birds and the wolves and all the animals are always the same and know nothing of borderlines? As far as I'm concerned, borders are something quite different…

The true borders, so her father had repeated to her during their journey together, are those between the powerful and the poor, between those who enjoy food and power and those who starve and have to break their backs for a fistful of polenta. Yes, those are the only true borders.

And if at that moment someone had asked her to give herself a name in this undertaking of hers, she would definitely have chosen Dandelion.

She rode her horse, thinking that her father and her whole family would be proud of her. Of course, it was not the first time she had done this, but it was the first time she had done it alone, and, as she entered this forest that plummeted down to the valley, she felt as if she had passed an important test.

She felt grown up, she felt she had become a real woman.

"Ya!" she said. "Let's go!"

12

S HE CONTINUED recalling her first journey, which allowed
her to get a better sense of her bearings and almost always
choose the right direction in which to go, the correct route that
would lead her to her destination.

She well knew that the first part of the descent would be
simple, interspersed as it was with larch forests and expanses
of firs and watered frequently by medium-sized brooks and
streams that were easy to cross.

And so it was. During the first hour of the descent, what
she had to deal with, more than the dangers and the wild ruggedness of the landscape, was the tiredness and the sudden
onsets of sleep, which by now were starting to gain the upper
hand. Samson looked exhausted, too, and even his stride grew
uncertain, as if he were ever more reluctant to proceed at the
same pace.

But things got noticeably worse when the larch and fir woods
were replaced by the terrible inclines and smooth overhanging
rocks that characterized the depths of the Noana Valley. This
valley was a genuine canyon, carved slowly out of the rock over
millions of years by the river of the same name.

All the streams and brooks she had encountered so far along
the way now flowed into a single, large stream that descended to

the bottom of the canyon with devastating force, with foaming rapids that produced waves as much as a couple of metres high.

It was an extraordinary sight for the eyes, but it was also a stretch of the journey that was so dangerous that it had put even her father's mettle and cool head to a hard test, almost bringing both him and Hector down.

"Tie his muzzle to that oak!" her father had yelled at her amid the din of the water plunging violently to the floor of the canyon.

Jole had taken the end of the rope and was wrapping it around the animal when a small landslide had caused Hector's forelegs to slide to the edge of the ravine.

"Damn!" Augusto had cried. "I'm falling!"

In two bounds, he had joined his daughter, torn the rope from her hand and in a moment had tied it around the tree, thus saving both the animal and the load.

"You have to be more careful and more alert!" he had yelled at her.

"Sorry, Papà."

"Remember, daughter. Earning a living is long, but dying is a moment." And saying this, he had stroked her head.

Jole returned to the present and tried to concentrate in order to stop herself from sliding. In a few moments, the fear and the adrenaline had swept away all her sleepiness, all the symptoms of fatigue, and she had regained the vitality and the speed of reflex of a squirrel when faced with danger.

Remaining on horseback, she gradually managed to find just the right slope leading down to the stream, which she would then have to follow for a few kilometres, until in its last stretch the valley opened out towards Imer and Mezzano.

It took Jole an immense effort to descend that damned rock face. After a while, she was forced to tie herself and the horse to the trunk of a huge oak at least three or four centuries old. The tree must have been waiting all that time for her to pass this way, she thought, just so that it could help her in this undertaking.

When at last she reached the right bank, held impressively tight within the hellish confines of the canyon, Jole suddenly felt her strength fail her. She sat befuddled on her horse, surrounded by the roar of the current, and looked up at the sky.

The sun was directly above her, and a flock of ravens hovered over her head with all the patience of those who know nothing of the passing of the seasons.

Her mouth was as dry as the bark of a spruce.

When she dismounted, she felt dizzy and her hands and feet suddenly lost all sensation. It seemed to her as if she had an ant's nest in her hair, and her forehead was beaded with cold sweat. As she tried to sit down, she fell to the ground, exhausted.

13

THEY WERE DINING on polenta, ricotta and cardoons. Agnese was sitting at the head of the table, in her husband's seat: he had been gone for more than a year. Jole was facing her, at the other end of the table, Antonia and Sergio on either side. Nobody spoke. The skin of their faces and hands was as brown and dry as a roebuck's horns. It was mid-September, and all four had laboured from dawn to dusk among the tobacco plants, gathering the leaves and putting them to soak and dry.

Agnese cut a slice of polenta with the twine and lifted it to her mouth, her eyes half-closed with tiredness.

"Mamma," Sergio suddenly said to her, "when is Papà coming back?"

Agnese opened her eyes wide and looked at Jole, then at the polenta, and finally at the crucifix hanging above the door post. The sun's last rays of the day came in through the window, pale and mild but still warm. The room smelt of mould and burnt firewood and tobacco.

Jole rose from her chair and went to put a log in the stove. Antonia took her plate and shuffled over to the window to look at a sunset that was sadder than usual.

"Papà is dead, isn't he?" Sergio asked.

"Don't say such things!" Agnese exclaimed. "Don't even think them!"

Then she rose, leaving her slice of polenta on her plate along with the cardoon leaves and a small handful of ricotta, and walked to the bedroom. Jole went to her little brother, looked him straight in the eyes and said, "If you love a person, that person is always there. Understand?"

"No," Sergio said. "I miss Papà so much, Jole."

Antonia came to them and felt the need to embrace them.

Outside, in the meantime, the sun's last rays came to rest behind the mountains, giving way to evening and then to deep night.

14

WHEN SHE REGAINED CONSCIOUSNESS, her head felt numb and her eyes, still half closed, could not yet make out the outlines of anything.

She seemed to see Samson's muzzle at close quarters and then had the strange sensation that the skin of her face was both damp and rough. She opened her eyes wide and realized that it was all true: the horse was licking her to revive her.

She wiped her face with her shirtsleeve and pulled herself up with difficulty, first raising her torso, then getting back on her feet. Cawing in a melancholy manner, a dozen ravens rose in flight from the branches of the surrounding lime trees. Samson neighed and laid his muzzle on Jole's right shoulder, and she stroked it. She felt as if she had slept for days, and she had a terrible headache. She looked up at the sky and noticed that the sun was where she had last seen it: above her head. She must have lost consciousness for only a few seconds.

She remembered her father. God alone knew when he had died, or where, or why. Even though he wasn't here, she always felt as if he were by her side, with those silences of his, those looks that were cautionary but also capable of expressing so much warmth. She dismissed the memory.

She relieved Samson of his load, placing it out of reach of the fine spray of water that continued emanating from the waterfall, and when she had finished she slapped the horse on the thigh to urge him into the stream at a point where the current was less strong.

Samson was thus able to free himself of the earth and the mud and the dust and the stale sweat, but also of the dozens of insects forever buzzing around him.

At this time of day and at this point in the canyon, totally sheltered from the wind and beaten fiercely by the sun that glared off the rocks of the two walls, it was very hot even though it was autumn. Jole walked to the river bank, a few metres downstream, where over the centuries the current had created a little cove that ended in a natural granite *cadino*, a pool of dark-blue water at least a metre deep. She washed her face and then, beginning with her boots, stripped completely, garment by garment, savouring the warmth of the sun on her smooth skin. She took a step forward and with her fingers skimmed the seductive surface of the water in the *cadino*. The skin all over her body, with the exception of her face and hands, was as bright as a lunar dawn, and the shivers gave her gooseflesh.

She closed her eyes, counted mentally to four, and on the count of five plunged into the water, which felt like recently melted snow.

She immersed herself in it entirely, disappearing into it, without thinking, the breath knocked out of her and her skin covered in goose pimples. Her muscles suddenly reawakened.

She came back up and opened her eyes. She felt as if she had been reborn, as if the tiredness and the pain, the bruises and blisters on her feet, every scratch and even every bad thought, every fear, had been swallowed by this miraculous water and dissolved in it for ever.

She stretched her legs. The water came up to her breast-bone. She stayed like this for a while, motionless, passing both hands through her wet hair. Then she skimmed her face with her palms, stroked her cheeks and lips and neck. She delicately touched her thighs and backside, and then, moving her hands up, her belly and her breasts. She continued touching herself in that blessed water, and the more aware she was of her woman's body beneath her hands and fingertips, the better she felt.

She remembered a young man she had seen a few months earlier at the marble quarries down in Sasso. For a moment, she thought he was there in front of her and imagined that the hands with which she was touching herself were actually his. He was handsome, tall, dark. She immediately dismissed the thought from her head.

She came out of the water, shivering as the last birch leaf remaining on a tree in December may shiver, and her wet hair was so long that it hung all the way down to the dimples above her buttocks. She made a dash for her things, took a hemp blanket and wiped herself as best she could. She whistled to Samson, who emerged in his turn from the stream and came up to her.

"You look at least two years younger," she said to him with a laugh.

She dressed, fanned her hair out on a rock exposed to the sun and waited for it to dry at least a little, then wetted the red kerchief in the stream and wrung it out, put it back around her neck, again loaded Samson from head to foot, put her hat on her head and her rucksack and rifle over her shoulder and set off again.

The last two hours of travelling through the Noana Valley were uneventful.

She was now near the Primiero Valley, from which two great Alpine spurs soared to the east, stretching all the way to the mines of Valtiberina and California.

She reached the gates of Imer at about four, after a journey of two and a half days and about sixty kilometres.

Remaining hidden in the forest, she needed before anything else to get her bearings, to remember the exact point where, three years earlier, she and her father had tied the mule Hector and hidden the entire load of tobacco.

She went down a few impracticable paths used by hunters and came to a crag beneath which was a dark wooden crucifix with a dying Christ looking down sadly at a deep ditch half-hidden by branches, most likely an *orsara*, one of those bear traps very common in these parts.

Jole did not remember that crucifix, which had probably been put there recently, but she did recall both the crag and the bear trap. She climbed again, in a south-westerly direction, and before long found herself in an impassable, labyrinthine forest. It had come back to her that her father had marked certain trees with his initials.

She dismounted, went back and forth like a mushroom

picker and at last found them: three spruce trees positioned like the vertices of an equilateral triangle, each side twenty metres long, with three letters clearly carved in the bark: ADB.

She hobbled Samson to one of the marked trees, went to the middle of the space and began searching through the autumn leaves, the moss, the weeds, the branches that had broken and fallen to the ground. After a few setbacks and hesitations, she finally unearthed what she was looking for: four planks of wood, corroded and eaten by termites.

With an effort she lifted them one at a time, bringing to light a big hole dug in the ground by her father and used as a hiding place for the load.

She smiled. She went back to Samson, gradually untied all the merchandise and hid it in the hole, one piece at a time, down to the last pouch of tobacco. Then she also deposited there everything she had been carrying in her clothes, hidden in pockets and folds and seams, and finally laid the planks back down to close up the hiding place.

It was only now that she noticed the sacred image. She found it by chance as she lifted one of the planks.

It was lying face down among the leaves at the rim of the hole: the image of St Martin that her father always carried with him, now discoloured and half-eaten by time and the dampness of the forest.

She reached out her hands, dirty with humus, took hold of it delicately and lifted it to her chest.

She wept, then plucked up her courage and tried to recover the clear-headedness that had helped her to get this far.

Before he died, she thought, *Papà must have come this way one last time.*

A series of questions without answers crossed her mind. Had that image been lost by her father accidentally, or had he left it there deliberately in the hope that sooner or later she would find it? What if he had been the victim of an ambush and killed on the spot? And finally, what if it had not been lost by Augusto but by someone else?

It took her only a moment to realize that this hiding place was no longer safe, and so, as the last light of day filtered obliquely through the branches and the first owls began to hoot, she decided to quickly find another.

She took the little shovel she had brought with her and moved breathlessly about a hundred metres further south, where she spotted another three spruces an equal distance one from the other, with a large toadstool in the middle.

Here, she started digging in the undergrowth, which smelt of late raspberries and poisonous mushrooms, until she had excavated a hole that was smaller than the other but large enough to contain everything.

She now went back to the first hole, lifted the planks again and took everything out, including the rifle. Two or three things at a time, she transferred the entire load to the new hiding place. Within less than an hour, she had deposited everything there. Everything except something to eat.

She covered the hole with topsoil, moss, leaves and pine branches and finally went to bring Samson, hobbling him tightly to a holm oak a few paces from her. Last of all, she took out the knife she carried at her waist and walked around the three spruce trees, one at a time. At the base of each trunk she carved the letters JDB.

Then she sat down to eat: three slices of old salami, black bread and a small piece of Morlacco.

She watched as a squirrel approached her then immediately changed its mind and quickly climbed a black pine.

She drank a very small amount of the water left in one of the two canteens and poured what was left into Samson's parched mouth.

"I'll be back soon," she whispered to him, stroking his muzzle.

As the orange-gold setting sun fragmented in the undergrowth into a thousand beams of bright light, she tied her hair, put her hat on her head, slipped her father's sacred image in her pocket and at last went down to the town, looking about her with the eyes of a lynx.

15

B EFORE LONG, she entered Imer.
The sun had only just disappeared behind the peaks of
the Lagorai, but the landscape was still illumined by its sharp
rays, which neatly divided the streets and houses of the town
into light and shade, and to the north, on the opposite side,
seemed to set the rocks of the Pala range ablaze in a stunning
alpenglow.

Jole walked down the alleys of beaten earth and cobbles
that led to the centre of the town and stopped in the main
square, by a fountain. She washed her hands and face, then
filled the canteen she carried tied to one of the belt loops of
her knickerbockers. A mongrel came up to her, wagging its
tail, stood up on its hind legs and licked her hands, which she
had placed on the stone rim of the fountain. She stroked its
head until a loud whistle called it away and it immediately
abandoned her and ran off into one of the adjoining alleyways.

She looked around suspiciously, even though reason told her
not to worry, since with the tobacco and the rifle well hidden
in the forest she had nothing to fear. All the same, it was best
to keep well clear of customs men and prying eyes.

She saw only four people in the street: an old shepherd walking along with a small flock of sheep and the dogs following on;

a young man chopping firewood in the doorway of his house; a woman coming towards the fountain with two big empty buckets; and a drunk leaning against the wall of a building singing out-of-tune songs about the beauty of the mountains and something else she could not catch.

At the far end of the street, Jole spotted two uniformed customs officers, but fortunately they vanished immediately down a side street. She sat there a moment or two longer, looking around while avoiding eye contact, with one foot propped on the rim of the fountain. She remained until just before the woman with the two buckets got there. By the time she had, Jole was already ten paces further on, and soon afterwards turned left into Pichler Strasse, a dark, squalid alley.

A black cat crossed her path, hissing, its tail held erect. Jole froze. Then she took a deep breath and continued walking, while the light of day faded moment by moment, giving way to the darkness of night. With each step she took, she heard ever more distinctly the noises and the cries of men coming from a specific point at the end of the alley.

She kept moving in the direction of those phlegmy, guttural noises, mostly made up of harsh consonants, until she came to a pearwood sign hanging on the wall to her left, on which the words *Black Bear Inn* had been branded.

Jole adjusted her hat, turned down the right corner of her mouth and narrowed her eyes in a grimace that was trying its best to look like a smug smile.

She had come to the right place, grim as it was. She was certain that it was here she would find the man she was looking for: Mario De Menech, who had always done business with her father in the past. She took a couple of deep breaths and went in.

Everything was shrouded in a dense half-light only slightly overcome by a dozen candles positioned on the tables and the walls, which cast the customers' grotesque shadows all over.

The first thing she was aware of was the overpowering stench of sweat and hops that assailed her nostrils.

Between her and the counter there must have been a dozen men, while to her right, where the inn's main room stretched all the way to the majolica *stube* dominating one whole corner at the far end, there must have been another thirty. Some of them were sitting at tables, busy drinking and playing cards, others thronged around the tables or leapt from one to another. If there was anyone without a tankard of beer in his hand, it was only because he had put it down for a moment.

Nobody was drinking wine.

Some were smoking, although not many, and sniffing the dense, heavy smoke that hung in mid-air throughout the inn, Jole observed that the tobacco rolled in the cigarettes was of poor quality. Probably Tyrolean or Bavarian—Kraut, anyway.

Jole noted the presence of many miners: they were easy to spot because they were physically much shorter than other men and their faces were black.

They were all chattering away, some in loud voices, some more quietly; there were those who cursed or quarrelled or became worked up over nothing, especially those who were losing at *Zeltwurm*, a card game similar to the *briscola* played in the Veneto. In general, the place was full of bustle and din and the host was struggling to keep up with every order.

On the walls, which were covered in strips of poor-quality matchboard, hung stuffed animals: the inevitable stags' heads with giant antlers, a grouse with its tail fanned open and its neck erect in the act of emitting a mating cry and even a marmot.

She looked at these animals with the same embarrassment with which she might have looked at her mother's naked body. She had no problem with shooting an animal. Killing was part of nature and the world, especially her world. What she found distasteful was exhibiting the corpses of murdered animals, turning them into trophies to be put on public display.

She made up her mind and edged closer to the middle of the room, over towards the counter.

She was genuinely beautiful, but fortunately in the general bustle nobody had noticed her, probably due to the gloom in which the room was shrouded, but also because she had her hair gathered inside her hat and was dressed like a peasant from the mountains of the south, who were generally poorer—insofar as it was possible to say which were the poorer mountain dwellers and which the richer, given that they were all poor wretches.

This was obviously the effect she hoped to obtain, in order to move with more confidence and make her way through, searching for De Menech's face among all these faces.

She examined many men out of the corner of her eye, pretending to look at something else and above all without ever remaining still for a moment, which would definitely have immediately attracted everyone's attention. She looked right and left and over to the far end. The inn was filled with vigorous, truculent faces, dishevelled heads on bloated bellies, young men who looked old and old men who looked like corpses, yellowed or rotten teeth, heavy breathing, swollen jaws heavy with capillaries ready to explode like a charge in the tunnels of the mines.

Jole held her breath for a moment and then focused on one man. It had to be him: De Menech. He was sitting at a table near the *stube*, playing *Zeltwurm* with two cronies who seemed shabbier than he was. She took a better look at him.

Time passed for everyone, and especially if you lived the kind of life De Menech lived three years are an eternity, and yet she had recognized him. Yes, she was sure of it: it really was De Menech.

Moving slowly, without lifting her gaze from the floor, she was approaching his table when she heard the front door slam behind her.

She turned.

Everyone turned and saw two officers of the Hapsburg army swagger in. One was about one metre eighty, the other slightly shorter. They were in full dress uniform, complete with regulation hats and flashes, pistols and bayonets in their belts.

No sooner had they made their entrance than almost everyone in the inn fell silent, even those with more beer in their bodies than the others.

Jole moved slowly towards the back of the room, trying not to attract attention to herself amid the natural motion of bodies and tankards. She pulled her hat down even further over her eyes, walked to the old majolica *stube*, grabbed a wooden chair and sat down on it with her back to the counter, on which the two soldiers were now leaning with their elbows.

From that position she could keep an eye on them without being seen by them.

"*Eine grösse spritz!*" the shorter of the two pronounced, addressing the host, a fat hirsute man the fingers of whose hands were as swollen and bright red as stag sausages.

"*Zwoa,*" the other added, in South Tyrolean dialect.

Then they laughed coarsely and said some things to each other that nobody could understand.

The host served them two large glasses two-thirds filled with white wine and a third with water.

From the singsong tone of their words, it was clear that the two officers were already in their cups.

They were thin and erect, and it was obvious that they were accustomed to military discipline. They both had thin, curled moustaches and every time one of them said something they both burst out laughing as if there were nobody else in the room.

Jole remained motionless, demonstrating a cool head. In the hope that the two men would leave as soon as possible, she killed time looking at the decorations on the *stube*, which must have been lit less than half an hour earlier because its tiles were only now starting to get warm.

She did not remember it at all and told herself she had never seen anything so beautiful, not even that time she had gone to Bassano with her father and visited the house of a rich gentleman to whom they had sold copper.

That powerful dignitary lived in part of a palace in the historic centre of the city, and in the main drawing room of his residence there was a huge old red-and-blue ceramic stove, decorated with floral patterns that at the time had seemed to her like waves of *botiro*, the butter her mother made in summer.

But the *stube* in the Black Bear Inn was much more beautiful.

On its green-and-white tiles, dozens of spectacular stag-hunting scenes were depicted in brown and yellow, placed in sequence from right to left and from bottom to top.

She looked at them spellbound, and as she followed the narrative thread she had the feeling that she was reading a story from beginning to end, even though she could barely read.

All at once, the two imperial soldiers drank one last toast to Austria and staggered noisily out into the street. Only then did the men inside the inn again start to make the usual racket, as if nothing had happened.

After a few moments, she stood up from the chair and moved gradually towards the man she had identified, until she was in front of him. At this point he looked up at her and said, "What do you want, boy?"

The other two, who were definitely miners, remained silent, concentrating on the cards they held in their hands and their foaming tankards of beer.

She took a closer look at him, and it struck her that he had grown brutish, like an animal that has lost all domestication.

Even those few teeth that three years earlier had still been attached to his gums were gone now. He had two new warts on the tip of his nose, his hands were covered in gnarled veins, there was a scar on his right cheek and his eyebrows were as thick as two box bushes.

For a moment, just from looking at him, she felt like vomiting.

"De Menech?" she asked, pushing her hat back slightly from her forehead.

He put his cards down on the table and took a closer look at her.

"I'm Jole De Boer, Augusto's daughter."

He gave a start and his mouth fell open. It took only a moment for the expression of incredulity carved on his features to soften and turn into one of sarcastic merriment.

"As you can see, I'm busy," he said brusquely. He picked up his cards and said something to the other two.

"I have to talk to you," Jole went on resolutely.

De Menech looked at her again and realized that she was serious.

He asked his cronies for permission to leave the game, got to his feet and, passing her without looking at her, whispered, "Follow me!" Saying this, he dragged his heavy body through a small opening that led into a darker room separate from the main room of the inn.

After a few moments she followed him, and once she had joined him they sat down at a table.

"Are you trying to get me into trouble?" he asked with an agitated air. "What are you doing here on your own?"

"What my father always came to do."

"So why didn't *he* come? Where is he?"

"I was hoping you could tell me that. My father left to come here two years ago, but never returned home."

De Menech listened to these words with incredulity, as if he knew nothing about it.

Jole studied him closely, trying to discern if he did actually know something about her father or, worse still, if he had something to do with his disappearance and death. But she could tell nothing. De Menech's face expressed only surprise and sorrow.

"Two years ago he left here with a whole lot of stuff, and last year he didn't show up again. I assumed that what he'd earned had been enough for him and that he'd decided to quit smuggling."

"Tell me the truth! Tell me what you know."

"I swear to God I don't know a thing," he said ingenuously. Then he looked her in the eyes and added, "I bet you're hungry, eh?"

Jole did not reply.

"Wait here a minute, I'll be right back."

He stood up and left the room.

She thought of the question he had asked her and felt her stomach rumble: she had not eaten anything hot for days.

After a few minutes, De Menech returned with a steaming plate of bean soup and a wooden spoon and put them down on the table in front of her.

"Lamon beans," he said. "Eat, it'll do you good."

Jole moved the plate closer to her, gobbled the beans down in a few seconds and carefully wiped the plate clean. The skin of her face relaxed a little.

De Menech began to look at her more closely and noticed that she had grown and, in growing, had actually become quite beautiful.

He looked at her lips and the swelling of her breasts gently pushing at the thick, coarse material of her jacket.

"How about a beer?" he asked in a more docile voice.

"Not now."

"You were here three years ago, weren't you?"

"Three years ago, yes."

"You were just a little girl then, and now look what a beautiful young lady you are!"

She stiffened. "Stop it!"

He laughed, but then turned serious. "I won't even think about it, but only out of respect for your father, may he rest in peace."

At these words, she pointed a threatening finger at him. "So you know he's dead! Tell me the truth!"

He grabbed her arm and twisted it. "You'd better calm down, girl, if you don't want them to hear us out there. Do you want to get us both into trouble?" Then he let go of her arm and continued, "Like I said, I don't know a damned thing about your father. I respected him a lot, he was a great man: strong, brave and honest. Losing his business was a real upset for me, don't you see that? I didn't have any reason to kill him, but someone else may have done, who can say? How should I know? I said may he rest in peace, didn't I? If he hasn't been home in two years, I doubt things are going too well for him right now. In the mountains either you live or you die, there's no middle way."

She took the holy image of St Martin from her pocket and put it down on the table in front of him. "This was his," she said. "I found it in the woods above Imer, just a few hundred paces from here."

"I swear to you, girl, I don't know anything about it."

"Maybe someone found out about the business the two of you were doing and—"

"Nobody ever found out anything, I can guarantee that. The miners who supplied me with copper and silver in return for his tobacco didn't know him and he didn't know them."

Jole calmed down and lowered her gaze, realizing that this man really did admire her father and that there was no reason for him to lie.

"The road back to your home is a long one," he said, "and the mountains and woods are full of criminals, you know."

"I hope you're telling me the truth."

"I am. But for now, speak quietly and tell me: you brought some tobacco with you, didn't you?"

"I don't know."

"Come on, if you're Augusto De Boer's daughter, you must have brought some, eh?"

She stared him in the eyes and said softly, "How much copper for a kilo?"

De Menech's eyes lit up like those of a child faced with a gift he has been dreaming about for two years. "A hundred grams," he replied.

"Not enough. My tobacco is worth much more."

"A hundred and twenty!" he said resolutely.

"Either two hundred or nothing."

He thought about it a moment and then said, "Not a gram more."

"And how much silver for a kilo?" she went on. He did not have time to respond before she proposed, curtly: "A hundred grams."

"But I can't!"

"It's that or nothing. I risked my life to come here."

With a snort, he gave up. "All right."

Jole could barely read, but she could count. She was silent for a few seconds and then said, "Get eight kilos of copper and four of silver ready for tomorrow."

De Menech, too, did some calculations, which left him flabbergasted, unable to say anything except, "Eight… eighty kilos of Brenta Valley?" And saying this, he opened wide his bloodshot yellow eyes.

"Give or take a gram."

"Damn! And what's it like?"

"Excellent, perfectly mature and very well dried. Shag and leaf, for snuff, for chewing and for smoking."

"Good!"

Still grave, Jole said, "Tomorrow morning."

"Yes," he said.

"Half an hour from here, on the way up to the Noana Valley, there's an old wayside shrine showing the three wise men bringing gifts to the baby Jesus."

"I know the place you mean, but take a good look at me: I don't like climbing."

"I'll see you there at dawn," she said without stooping to compromise or argument.

"But I don't know if between now and then I can get together all that—"

"It's that or nothing, I can't stay here any longer."

"All right. It won't be easy, mind you. These days, it's like all the customs officers in the Hapsburg Empire have woken up. The place is full of police and soldiers, damn them... Did you say something?"

"No, I didn't say anything."

"Oh, I thought—"

"Eight of copper and four of silver," she repeated. "That's the only thing I had to say to you."

De Menech looked around furtively and then, taking one of her arms and moving his face innocently close to hers, whispered, "The Krauts may be good at making cannon, but they should leave tobacco-making to you people from the Veneto."

"So is it a deal?" she said.

"It's a deal. Your father would be proud of you, girl."

They shook hands, then left the room as inconspicuously as possible.

She went first, and he followed a minute later.

16

D E MENECH could count on seven trusted men who worked for him and with whom he did business.

They were workers who surreptitiously swallowed the metals in the tunnels and then recovered them at home, carefully sifting through their own faeces. In the tunnels and outside the mines, there were always imperial inspectors who had the task of searching the miners at the end of their shifts, which made hiding anything quite impossible, since it would be impossible to evade their stringent checks. That was why the safest thing was to hide the copper and silver inside your own body, the most secret place of all.

The most trusted and the most productive of De Menech's men was named Sepp Näckler, and it was he who supplied the merchandise for the De Boers.

Näckler was about fifty years old. He had been born and raised in the South Tyrol, in a village near Tiers, and had ended up working in the Primiero mines after a life filled with criminal activities. At the age of twenty he was incarcerated in the imperial prison in Innsbruck for molesting a child, and after being subjected to every kind of torture was sent to work in the mines as a "marmot", the nickname given to those with the task of setting off explosive charges in the tunnels.

He was short and tiny, with bulging eyes that looked as if they were trying to leave their sockets. He had a sharp nose and was affected with acute scoliosis, which over time had curved and hunched his back until he looked like a Saxon wood troll. He never spoke, perhaps because he had nothing more to say.

For twelve years he had been working alternately in the Val Canali mine and the Canalet mine, scraping off copper and silver, swallowing a little every week and hiding it at home, running the risk of being hanged in the square named after the emperor.

He lived with another man, a miner who shared his life of poverty and also his secret. They resided in a log cabin just outside Imer, a few minutes' walk from the wooden crucifix that had recently been put up near the *orsara* above the town.

There was almost nothing in their cabin, and yet they had managed to set up and equip a little clandestine cast-iron smelting furnace, in which they cast and then solidified all the granules, fragments, powder and chips of silver and copper recovered from their faeces.

On behalf of De Menech, whom he had met years before at the Black Bear Inn, Näckler ate and shat copper, ate and shat silver, but had no real idea of their true market value.

Which is why De Menech regularly paid him back in prostitutes, as well as food and, every now and again, his much-coveted tobacco: as much tobacco as Näckler could smoke, chew and take as snuff for a whole year.

17

THE MINING DISTRICT of Primiero consisted of ten areas of excavation, all of considerable importance, and in addition to these mines there were others that were of lesser value but still quite productive. The richest in metals were definitely those of Val Canali, at the foot of Castel Pietra, from which copper was extracted, and Canalet, near Siror, from which abundant quantities of silver were obtained.

Apart from the most precious metals, siderite, barytes, galena and chalcopyrite were also present in all the mines. Overall, there were about a hundred tunnels, almost all of them fully operational, giving work to almost seven hundred people, men and boys. They all relied on a foundry situated in a nearby town called Forno, where a large furnace and several small forges worked the metals extracted in the area.

The workers employed in the mines of the Primiero Valley, like all miners throughout the world, were the very image of damned souls, expelled from hell and exiled on earth, without hope.

They were physically small and hunchbacked, their faces scorched from the constant explosions set off to make openings in the tunnels in search of new seams, with the dishevelled hair and dazed eyes of those who cannot tell if they are still alive or already dead.

Jole had never seen them at work, she had never been in a mine, but her father Augusto had. Once, standing with De Menech just outside one of the tunnels of the Colsanto mine, a few kilometres from Imer, he had seen these men condemned to work twenty hours a day in the innards of the world, the belly of the earth. Men hidden from life. Forced to lead an existence deprived of air, light, sky, stars. More like demons than human beings.

Augusto had seen dozens of them emerge from that hole that seemed to be ejecting them, spitting them out, spewing them from the depths. He had seen them move slowly and silently like ghosts and had thought about those poor unfortunates who, in an attempt to survive, tried to scrape a little metal from the bowels of the earth and take it into their own bowels.

And he had immediately felt Christian compassion. They were his brothers, men who, like him, were forced by hunger and suffering to do things they would never have done with a little more bread on the table: to deceive the customs men, the laws, the powerful, the king.

These miners had no hope, no future, not even a present.

Some of them, though, had managed one way or another to join the black market in copper, silver, iron, pyrite and lead.

18

Näckler managed to hide a reasonable quantity of metals every year, and when Jole De Boer arrived in the area in the autumn of 1896, De Menech knew that he would be able to satisfy the girl's requests. Indeed, Näckler had only just put several kilos of copper and silver away in a safe place.

As far as he was concerned, everything that resulted from his business with De Menech was going well. All he needed was a little amusement for his mouth, his throat and his penis.

Especially the latter, given that finding a woman willing to go to bed with him was practically impossible.

19

Swiping a handful of walnuts from a large bowl on the counter, Jole quickly left the Black Bear Inn, and without wasting any more time walked back up Pichler Strasse. There was a large moon in the sky, lighting up the walls of the houses, the surrounding woods and, at the far end of the valley, the wonderful Mount Cimone.

She walked confidently back to the main square and from there moved away from the town, climbing back up to the forest where she had left her things.

When he saw her, Samson whinnied with joy.

"Shh!" she said, raising her right index finger to her mouth and stroking him. "Here!" And she fed him the walnuts, duly shelled.

It was cold and damp, and the forest was full of bracken and broad leaves of meadow dock, which she called *lavàz* and which her grandmother had used to wrap fresh ricotta.

Everywhere there was a mild, delicate scent of crocuses, lichen and juniper berries.

A strange sudden gust of wind, apparently innocuous, rustled the foliage of the forest, announcing that the weather would soon change.

She took off her hat and removed the string that had fastened it, then, aided by the moonlight, recovered her blankets and rifle from the hole and lay down next to Samson, preparing to sleep propped up on the south side of a silver fir's thick trunk.

"Not much longer now," she said to Samson, and closed her eyes. There were a thousand thoughts in her head, swinging back and forth between feelings of nostalgia and a sense of foreboding. "If all goes well, we'll be going home tomorrow, which is All Saints'."

This was the night when the dead were worshipped, at least in the traditions of her mountains. She shuddered and recited a Requiem Æternam for her dear departed and a special one for her father.

A few hours later, when she had already been sleeping for a while, she was woken by some very strange noises. She thought at first it was a dream and turned immediately onto her other side, but after a few minutes she realized that this lugubrious dirge, this incomprehensible vocalise that sounded like a collective prayer, but a prayer such as she had never heard, was no dream, not even a nightmare. She sat up, then immediately got to her feet and grabbed her rifle.

The voices came from some way behind her. She turned and looked past the silver fir against which she had been sleeping, and there, beyond the forest, she glimpsed a light, a kind of orange lantern, then another, and finally a series of such lights, all identical, advancing in single file accompanied by a grim, chilling chorus, like the voices of evil spirits, of witches. So fearful was this chanting that Jole felt her blood freeze in her veins.

Clutching St Paul for comfort, ready to fire, she stayed hidden behind the tree, with the awful feeling the procession was coming her way—or at least that was the impression she had.

She tried to get a better look, while the dirge echoed ever more loudly through the forest, coming ever more relentlessly towards her.

Now they were within a hundred metres of her, and thanks to the lights of their lanterns she was able to see them more clearly.

She was terrified, her heart in her throat.

The group comprised both men and women, and thanks to what they were holding in their hands she managed to make out their faces. At this point she realized that those lighted objects were not lanterns, but hollowed-out pumpkins in which they had put torches.

Suddenly a long-eared owl rose from a branch above her head and flew towards the procession. Then Jole saw another, soon joined by an owlet and a barn owl.

All these birds had flown straight for the group of men and women, who now stopped and arranged themselves in a circle, ceasing their terrifying chorus and beginning to emit distressing, guttural sounds.

They lit a fire inside the circle and started dancing and shouting, although it was not clear whether their cries were of excitement or of suffering.

Once, as a little girl, she had met a woman in the woods near Stoner. This woman, who was gathering medicinal herbs, was tiny and almost toothless, and without Jole having said anything to her, she had talked to her of the witches' sabbath, and had also said that you had to be careful not to meet the eyes of certain people on the night of 31 October. Then she had vanished, just as time would later erase her from Jole's memory.

Now, though, at this instant of terror, the woman came back into her mind, as bright and timely as an object long lost and recovered at the right moment.

With all the fortitude she could find within her heart, Jole begged Samson not to make any noise. She remained frozen behind her tree with the rifle in her hand.

For two hours, she stood and listened to all the disturbing cries emerging from the mouths of those possessed beings.

Then at last it all ended, the people went away and peace was restored to the forest.

Never in her life had she heard or seen anything like it.

20

ON LEAVING the Black Bear Inn, De Menech calmly returned home, stayed there a good half hour making calculations then took his white donkey from the stable and slowly rode out of the town in the direction of Näckler's cabin. He found him busy cutting into an orange pumpkin, as if trying to carve out two eyes, a nose and a mouth. Stopping between incisions to see how his strange task was coming along, he would knock back generous swigs of home-made pine grappa, while an emaciated, bristly-haired, flea-ridden cat miaowed insistently behind a chair stuffed with straw.

"What would you say to a bit of tobacco, you old bastard?" De Menech asked him from the door.

Näckler grinned in a devilish fashion, then turned and exhibited a smile as eloquent as it was monstrous.

De Menech entered the cabin and closed the door behind him with the heavy, rusty chain that hung on the wall.

He sat down and accepted a little grappa.

He took a swig straight from the bottle and wiped his mouth with his fustian shirtsleeve.

"Give me eight pieces of copper and four of silver, and tomorrow I'll bring you twenty kilos of the best tobacco!"

Näckler gave that devilish grin again and hissed something that resembled "Good or bad?"

"Tobacco from the Veneto. You know it well. The best in all Europe. For two years now, it's been impossible to find even a gram of it around here."

"Twenty?"

"Twenty. But you have to give me the pieces now, I know you have them."

The ragged cat miaowed loudly, as if trying to join in their conversation.

Näckler left the cabin, returned ten minutes later with a jute sack on his back and put it down right in front of De Menech.

While waiting, De Menech had grabbed hold of the bottle. Without saying a word, Näckler pointed to it, then immediately went back to work on his pumpkin.

Calmly, De Menech drank, looked smugly at Näckler, belched, then went and picked up the sack, which had been left a few paces from him.

He opened it and counted the pieces: it was the right number.

"Now get out," Näckler said, stroking the black cat. "I have things to do tonight."

21

O N THE EVENING of 2nd November 1894, Agnese had
gathered her children and led them into her bedroom
and over to the image of the Madonna hanging in the corner.
Two months had passed since Augusto had left, and he had
not returned. He should have been away for just a few days,
long enough to effect the usual exchange, but he had not
come home.

Agnese had asked Jole, Antonia and Sergio to hold each
other by the hand, had taken the rosary she kept hidden in
an old yew chest and had begun praying.

"Virgin Mary," she had said, "let us leave the worship of
the dead to the Evil One, and as good Christians let us instead
commemorate the departed. Amen."

"Amen!" her children had responded in unison.

"De profundis clamavi ad te, Domine, exaudi vocem meam…"

"Amen!"

Jole had been bewildered by these words that meant nothing to her. Deep down, even her mother did not understand
what they meant but repeated them from memory like the
cry of a thrush, because thus it was written and thus it had
been transmitted from generation to generation. To Jole, it
had seemed as if the image of the Madonna and the room

and the trees outside and the whole world were all a kind of waking dream, a heavy, hopeless dream into which she had felt herself sinking, even though her mother's strength and faith were unshakeable.

"*Requiem æternam dona eis, Domine, et lux perpetua luceat eis. Requiescant in pace.* Amen."

"Amen!"

Jole had looked down at the floor and noticed a little spider between her shoes. She had wondered what it meant to be such a small animal, what life was like for that tiny creature.

"Have you ever missed anyone?" she had asked it under her breath.

To avoid stepping on it, she had picked it up and taken it outside, while the others continued to pray.

Just outside the front door, she had put it down on the stack of firewood.

"Go," she had said. "And hope you never have to die."

22

AFTER WHAT SHE HAD SEEN, Jole was unable to get back to sleep.

In those few hours the weather had changed, and a heavy blanket of damp had fallen like a cloak over the woods and the whole valley. An hour and a half before dawn, she hurried to the secret hiding place with Samson, took out what she had hidden there and loaded it, one thing at a time, on her loyal travelling companion's powerful back. Then she set off, crossing the forest in the direction of the arranged meeting place, which was less than an hour away.

I can't wait for this whole thing to be over and done with. Jesus, if you're there, listen to me! I can't wait to lie down in the meadow in front of our house and listen to the song of the chaffinches. I can't wait to drink a bowl of warm milk and watch the clouds drifting over our woods. I can't wait to close my eyes and not have to open them out of fear. I can't wait to have a true shelter, a protection, a certainty. I can't wait to be at home and at peace, to be embraced by my family, to caress my mother. I hope it all goes well, just as it has gone well until now. But the truth is, I'm afraid. I'm so afraid.

She still shuddered at the thought of the witches' sabbath and wondered what could possibly lead some men and some women to perform rituals like that.

Riding Samson, she lightly touched one of her trouser pockets to make sure her little wooden horse was there. She felt safer, and she prayed to St Martin, whose image she also kept in her pocket, to protect her.

She was the first to reach the shrine of the three wise men, and there she waited for De Menech.

The serene sky of the previous days was a distant memory. The whole of the Primiero Valley, including the surrounding mountains and the ascent leading to the Noana Valley, was covered over with low, enveloping clouds heavy with humidity, bringing Jole's face out in tiny drops of sweat.

Heaps of white clouds moved rapidly from one side to the other of the surrounding woods, as if bouncing here and there, hiding now one forest, now another, in some kind of Dolomite magic trick.

After a while, as dawn broke, De Menech appeared in the meadow below, gradually emerging from the last fog of the night like the shadow of a ghost, on the back of his white donkey, which was all saddled and harnessed and advancing very slowly, as if there were no tomorrow but only a task to be done in the here and now.

Reaching the shrine, De Menech greeted Jole with an upward jerk of his head.

"Let's be quick about it!" she immediately said.

"Slow down," he replied, calmly getting off the donkey.

He came and stood in front of Jole, lifted the dark cloak in which he was completely wrapped and took out a small assay balance.

Jole had expected this, it was only right that it should be so. "The tobacco!" he said.

She dismounted and, still keeping the rifle within easy reach, took out everything, laying every case and pouch on a hemp sheet to avoid their getting any damper than they already were.

Wasting no time, he weighed everything, with quick, practised gestures. It was all so fast that Jole was unable to follow his movements with any precision. But she did not miss the grimace on De Menech's face when he had finished the weighing, and she did not like that at all.

"It's not right, is it?" he said tersely.

She could feel the sweat on her hands. "What?"

"My balance says it's forty kilos in total, not eighty! I'll give you four kilos of copper and two of silver. That's only fair."

"It's eighty! Weigh it all again!"

"I'm not weighing anything again, I'll give you what you deserve, girl."

In a rapid move, she grabbed the rifle, aimed it at De Menech and cocked it. "If you don't give me the kilos we agreed, I'll be the one to give you what you deserve!"

De Menech stood there frozen. He had not expected anything like this. With the barrel of St Paul aimed at his forehead, all he could say was, "All right, it's eighty. But put down the rifle, girl."

"I'm not putting down a damned thing," she said, still keeping him in her sights. "And if you don't think I'd have the courage to shoot someone like you, all you have to do is put me to the test. I mean what I say."

He took from the donkey the jute sack Näckler had given him and removed the twelve pieces of metal: eight of copper and four of silver.

"Here they are," he said.

"Step forward, I want to see them properly!"

He moved half a metre forward and showed them to her. She nodded.

"Now weigh them in front of me, one at a time."

Calmly, De Menech did as he was told, moving slowly so that there should be no doubt.

"Good," Jole said. "Now load the sack on my horse, take the tobacco, get on your donkey and go. Until I see you vanish into the fog you came out of, I swear I'll be aiming the rifle at your head. Don't think I'm joking. I'm no man, I'm a woman!"

He gathered all the tobacco in its individual cases, bags, leather pockets and jute pouches and loaded them on the donkey, which brayed as if it had no intention of burdening itself with these eighty kilos.

"Goodbye!" she said.

"Why, aren't you coming back?"

"I don't know, but for now, goodbye!"

He smiled as if to tease her. "You'll be back, you'll be back," he sneered as he took up the donkey's reins. "I need your tobacco, and you need my copper and my silver."

"We'll see."

"One last thing," he added before setting off back down the slope towards the valley.

"Go on!"

"About your father. I'm sorry about this, but I didn't tell you the whole truth."

Jole's hands started sweating with anxiety and the rifle grew slippery.

"Please don't misunderstand me," he went on, slowly. "I have nothing to do with it and I don't know anything, but the fact is, I did hear something about him… although I don't believe it for a moment."

"What?"

"Well, they say that a couple of years ago, having come down here on the usual smuggling expedition, he met a pretty girl in the woods, more or less your age. Her name was Cecilia Mos, and she was from Canal San Bovo, a village not far from Imer. Well, you know how it is… They say he couldn't stop himself, if you know what I mean. First he had his fun, and then he killed her."

Jole felt a lump in her throat and realized that her nerves were so on edge she might well burst into tears.

"It's not true!" she cried. "It's all lies! And what's it got to do with his death anyway?" She was sobbing now, trying desperately to keep the rifle still and aimed at De Menech.

"What it's got to do with it," he replied, "is that the girl's father made him pay for what he'd done and killed him like a dog. That's what it's got to do with it. Although it's all rumour, of course!"

"You're nothing but a liar!"

"It's what people are saying," he said, sure of himself, as if he was now accustomed to having that rifle aimed at him.

"Get out of here!" she cried threateningly.

"I'm going, I'm going," he said with a snigger, gradually moving further and further away. "See you next year!"

After a few moments, he vanished into the dense haze of a cloudy dawn that was now beginning to lighten the surrounding landscape.

She counted to fifty, then lowered the rifle.

She checked the bars of copper and silver once again, tied around her horse's abdomen the laces of the bags where they would remain hidden and at last mounted Samson, who for once didn't have all those flies on his coat.

"Ya!" she said to urge him. "We're going home!"

PART THREE

1

RIDING AT A CONSTANT PACE, Jole began her return journey. She climbed back up the mountainside until she reached the pass, from where a trail branched off leading south-west, towards the Noana Valley.

After crossing a last section of conifer forest, she entered the broad mouth of the canyon and followed the course of the river. As she proceeded, the walls of the valley became ever steeper and narrower.

When the man reached the shrine, the girl must have only just left, certainly less than an hour ago, since on such a damp morning the hooves of her Haflinger were still imprinted in the muddy ground, and for someone like him the tracks were easy enough to follow.

He looked up, attracted by the repeated cry of an eagle that was beginning its hunt, then spurred his black horse and set off in pursuit.

Jole stopped near the *cadino* where she had bathed the previous day. Beneath those dark clouds, the water had lost its deep-blue colour and looked merely grey.

She looked around. It seemed like a completely different place.

The sky was clearing a little, but a few dark clouds still drifted by, moving at a constant speed.

It was cold and she took one of her woollen blankets, made a tear in the middle and put it on like a poncho. Samson drank from the stream, and some ten metres further upstream Jole filled the canteens. She had the feeling she had passed this way, not twenty-four hours ago, but weeks, if not months earlier!

She took a sip of the icy water and looked at the steep wall over which she would have to climb to get out of the valley. On foot, she ascended the long granite wall and tied her thick hemp rope to the trunk of a great elm, then came back down, mounted Samson and began the difficult ascent.

In the meantime, the usual flock of ravens had gathered nearby, perched on the branches of the higher ash trees in the hope of feeding on a human corpse or horse carrion. When she saw them she waved playfully at them.

"I made it on the way out," she said to them out loud, "and I'll make it now, too."

Despite her fatigue, the difficulties of the moment and her awareness of having to concentrate metre after metre on the return journey, she could not get what De Menech had told her about her father out of her head. It was impossible to dismiss those awful words from her mind, and they continued to ring in her ears and echo in her temples like a malignant, obsessive mantra, a black-magic spell that led to madness.

She could not believe that version of events. She was certain that the bastard had made it all up, just to see her suffer, to kill her inside.

But now her tiredness was really making itself felt, her strength was worn down to the bone, and her head and nerves, too, had grown fragile. She had been unable to sleep during the night and the previous day had been back-breaking, not to mention the fact that she had now been travelling for four days in extreme conditions. By now, despite her great determination, even the smallest effort was proving to be beyond her physical capabilities. Given all this, it was hardly surprising that De Menech's words, however hard she tried to ignore them, were slowly coming to dominate her thoughts.

The man continued to follow the horse's trail until the muddy ground was completely replaced by grassy pastureland. Samson's hoof tracks now disappeared, but for someone like him it was easy to guess the route the girl had chosen. If she wanted to get to the border, she would have to get through the narrow canyon of the Noana Valley and head straight for Mount Pavione, the only point on the border with Italy where patrols were almost non-existent, given the altitude and the treacherous conditions of that mountainous terrain. He smiled on seeing the tufts of grass flattened by her passing and continued on his way, riding his black horse.

*

After a few unsuccessful attempts, mainly due to the crumbly, slippery pebbles that had almost toppled Samson off a crag a dozen metres high, Jole at last made it.

Once she had reached the top of the granite wall, she untied the rope, retrieved the end of it and tied it as usual around Samson's harness.

She heaved a sigh of relief, drank and set off again.

Then he, too, reached the entrance to the canyon, where the waterfall thundered down, forming deep *cadini*. On the bank of the stream, he noted that the tracks of that slow, heavy horse had reappeared.

He was pleased with himself. He had not forgotten his hunting skills.

He, too, saw the ravens perched on the highest branches of the ash trees. He looked them up and down: they were enemies that would always lose against him.

He, too, looked in awe at those granite walls and wondered how he would climb them.

He, too, made it.

And he, too, had a rifle. A repeating Steyr Mannlicher.

Jole climbed through the dense undergrowth of broad-leaved trees and penetrated the level forest that surged towards the north side of Mount Pavione, which appeared and disappeared ahead of her like a dream that continued to deny itself. She and Samson zigzagged between the huge trunks of silver firs that must have been at least a hundred years old.

Along the route, she had easily crossed the many brooks and streams she had first encountered on the way out, proceeding over terrain that until the day before had been covered by a layer of tall moss as soft as cotton wool. Now it had become much muddier and swampier, and Samson's legs kept sinking into it.

The man came to that same forest through which she had passed no more than half an hour earlier.

He was gaining ground.

He looked at the peak of Mount Pavione glittering between the branches of the spruces and rising like a Titan. He would definitely catch up with her, but he told himself he would have to hurry to do so before the border. Not that it would be very different beyond the border, not for his purpose.

But catching up with her before she crossed would be better.

2

JOLE NOW FACED the long ascent that led to the border on Mount Pavione, still careful to make sure that there were no men from the *Zollwache* anywhere about. She constantly looked in front of her, and to her right and her left. Every two hundred metres, she stopped Samson and cocked an ear to catch any possible suspicious noises.

Gradually, she left the conifer forest behind her and plunged into meagre stands of larches and constant thickets of Swiss pine, which within a few minutes gave way to the vast scree of the highest mountain in the Vette Feltrine.

In a landscape like this, it was much easier to spot dangers ahead, but at the same time it was even easier to be spotted. She stopped to look carefully in front of her at the point she would have to reach at the top of the ridge, a gap at least five hundred metres from where she was now. A short-toed eagle was circling above her head, halfway between the mountain's rocky wall and slopes that were partly stony and partly green. The sun was shining again, and the wind that Jole had encountered once before in this vicinity now resumed blowing, emitting those unmistakable sounds that seemed like human voices. The soul of the border, its spirit, was once more greeting her with its loud voice.

She advanced without stopping for an hour and then, midway through the ascent—in other words, almost at the invisible border with Italy—she decided to stop and rest her horse.

They squatted behind a bush of mountain pine, surrounded by that sea of sharp stones and dandelions: those flowers that were never afraid.

It was early afternoon, and the mountains seemed asleep. She took out one of the two canteens and drank, unaware of anything untoward.

The man had stopped his horse quite a while earlier and had proceeded on foot, silently, very close to her, taking shelter behind a bush every time she stopped and looked around.

Now he came from below and pointed his rifle at her, taking her by surprise.

"Got you!" he cried.

She turned abruptly and saw a stranger dressed in black, ready to shoot her.

There was not even time to wonder if it was a hallucination before he repeated, "Got you!" This time he said it in a harsh tone full of hatred and contempt.

Jole was motionless, unable to say a word, her heart racing with fear.

"You're De Boer's daughter, aren't you?"

She did not understand any of this, let alone the meaning of that question. It seemed only natural to answer in the affirmative, and she nodded her head up and down.

The black-clad man took a few steps forward, his rifle still trained on her.

"That bastard raped and murdered my only daughter. Cecilia was just sixteen."

She swallowed air, and her mouth became as dry as the scree around her.

Everything lost colour, including the walls of the mountains and the dandelion flowers. Everything faded before her eyes. Every light was snuffed out the moment she heard those words.

"I swore to avenge my daughter and that's what I'm here for. When I saw you outside the Black Bear, I immediately knew who you were. I would have known even if De Menech hadn't confirmed it this morning and told me where I could find you."

She was incapable of moving, feeling as if she were paralysed from head to foot.

The wind was blowing hard, and she closed her eyes as if to listen to its voice, as if to hear whether there were any words for her coming from the sky: they would definitely be the last words she would hear in her life. All at once, though, she felt the rough surface of a stone under the palm of her hand. It was sharp and angular. That stone helped her to think again, like a spark capable of reigniting a fire now extinguished.

The man came even closer, and she could smell the stench of goat on his black clothes. Making sure she was not seen, Jole ran her hand over the stone and realized that it was big enough to be seized in a single move and small enough to be thrown at a decent speed.

The man said something she did not understand, then cocked his rifle, ready to sate his thirst for blood.

And at the very moment he uttered the word "revenge", Jole flung the stone at his head with all the strength she had.

It took a moment.

The stone struck the man in the right temple, and he fell to the stony ground like a chamois brought down by a hunter. In an agitated state, she immediately leapt to her feet and, seeing that he was lying there lifeless, his face covered in blood, she quickly gathered her things, mounted Samson and resumed her ascent towards the ridge.

After some fifty paces, she summoned the courage to turn and thought she saw the man's legs move and his head turn from side to side.

"Ya!" she cried to Samson. "Ya!"

Within a short time she had reached the pass. The usual wind that never stopped blowing up here was howling words of fear and flight that echoed like promises of revenge.

3

THE DESCENT on the Italian side was far from easy.

Jole was in a confused state, her mind filled with anxiety and terror, and Samson, sensing these moods, grew nervous, too. Jole knew that sooner or later the man would get back on his feet and resume his pursuit of her, just as she knew that her one hope of escaping him was connected with reaching the woods further down the mountain, where she would be certain to shake him off and there was no chance he would spot her again.

I have to make it, I have to make it, she said to herself. *Be brave, Jole! I have to hold out, chase away the fear, be strong, I owe it to myself and my family. That bastard mustn't catch up with me.*

More than once, Samson showed indecision, digging in with his forelegs or else making sudden movements which almost threw Jole several times.

After a thousand strains and hesitations, constantly looking behind her, Jole managed to get across almost the whole of the scree. It took more than an hour, but at last she reached the first pines below.

Metre by metre, the slopes grew gentler and the terrain ever softer and grassier, but just when it seemed that the situation was under control, Samson suddenly reacted as if possessed.

He reared up on his hind legs, neighing repeatedly. Jole lost her balance and fell, her backside hitting the ground hard.

She immediately felt her breath knocked out of her by the pain, cursed and wondered what could have happened to Samson. Trying to raise herself, she saw that there was a large viper in front of the horse, coiled in a threatening position. She grabbed a stone on her right and threw it at the reptile, hitting it just enough to make it slither away quickly between the brambles of a juniper thicket.

Samson calmed down immediately and brought his muzzle close to Jole. In the meantime, she had made an attempt to sit up in spite of the sharp pain in her back.

She remained in that position for a few minutes, trying to catch her breath, even though she could feel terrible spasms in her ribcage that were stopping her from taking deep breaths.

She struggled to her feet, walked around Samson and then, very calmly, remounted. She looked behind her to see if Mos was already on her trail, then nervously resumed her journey.

As she descended the mountainside, she kept thinking about the man in black who had ambushed her and how lucky she had been to escape him.

It was that bastard De Menech! It was he who betrayed me, telling him where he could find me and kill me... Mos. That was the man's name, wasn't it?

Above all, she kept thinking about what both men had told her about her father, those terrible words louder than rifle shots.

So it's true, she told herself as she anxiously rode Samson, *it's true that Mos killed my father out of revenge... But my father couldn't have raped and killed a girl, it's impossible.*

Proceeding more slowly now, she began crying.

Oh, my God, I'm lost. I've come all this way, and it's been for nothing.

By the time it reached her lips, every tear that streaked down her face had the bitter taste of misery, of total defeat, the inevitability of eternal hatred, the evil that ruled and would for ever continue to rule the world of men.

She repeatedly looked back and prayed to the Madonna even though she did not believe in her, uttering familiar words from memory, words taken for granted, words devoid of real meaning. They emerged warm from her heart and were ice-cold by the time they reached her mouth.

Once I'm back home, if I ever do get back, it won't be easy for me to go on living. How will I be able to tell my family any of this?

It was in this despondent state that she came to a secluded clearing protected by the south side of Mount Pavione and used as pasture for the flocks of sheep that came back down to the valley bottom at this time of year. She decided to stop for a while before resuming her journey.

She felt safe here, although not completely. It was mid-afternoon by the time she set up camp. Although her back hurt, there could not have been anything broken because she could move quite well. Samson immediately began to graze placidly on the highest tufts of grass sticking up from the ground.

She was hungry, but had nothing left to eat, or to drink.

The usual thoughts were moving about in her mind.

She took a deep breath but it hurt her: the jolt she had got in falling from her horse had been a strong one.

She closed her eyes and listened to the total silence that enveloped her.

I feel like a pine needle in an anthill, like a blade of grass in a prairie, like a small stone in the middle of the scree I just came through on Mount Pavione.

She opened her eyes again. There in front of her was the mountain, and she looked at it the way her mother looked at the high altar during Easter mass.

With trepidation, loyalty, fatal attraction, submission, passion and awe.

The mountain was lit up by the warm early-November sun and to Jole's eyes it seemed so calm and impassive, and yet so powerful, so treacherous, so formidable.

As only mountains can be.

As only some mountains can be.

4

WHEN SHE TURNED to the other side she saw in front of her a young woman who had sprung up all of a sudden without making any noise. Caught by surprise, Jole took fright. She tried to get to her feet, with difficulty because of the shooting pains in her back.

"It's all right, don't be afraid!" the unknown woman said. "I'm a shepherdess."

She was tall and her face was dirty, as were the rags she wore as clothes.

A hat made from the fur and tail of a fox covered most of her hair, although a few black strands fell over the back of her neck.

Behind her, a pair of spotted long-haired dogs appeared, and then a flock consisting of about a hundred Feltrina sheep.

"My name's Maddalena," she said, coming closer to Jole and confidently sitting down next to her. "You're the first woman I've met up here in many months."

She had dark, gentle eyes, and the look in them immediately reassured Jole.

"What's your name?" she asked.

"Jole De Boer. I come from a village above the Brenta Valley, near the Asiago plateau."

"What do you need that rifle for?"

"Nothing."

Maddalena opened the bag she had on her back, took out some fresh cheese, a canteen full of water and some rusks and handed them all to Jole.

Jole's eyes opened wide. She thanked her and shyly started eating and drinking, at last able to quench her thirst.

"What are you doing here?" Maddalena asked her.

"Running away," she said, promptly rising again, ready to go on her way.

"Running away? What from?"

"From a black man with a black horse... and my nightmares."

"When a lamb is lost on the mountains, it bleats loudly. Sometimes a wolf comes, but sometimes its mother comes."

Jole looked at her in bewilderment, as if she had not understood her words.

The shepherdess said nothing else but looked at her with a gleam of compassion in her eyes.

She gave her more cheese and rusks and embraced her.

It seemed to Jole that there was something sisterly in that embrace, and she felt a sense of profound comfort, a regenerative warmth in her heart that made her melt in Maddalena's gentle, affectionate arms.

The shepherdess picked a dandelion from the ground and delicately placed it between Jole's hair and right ear.

"Always remember that you have to be strong," she said, looking straight into her watery eyes.

Jole felt a strange sensation, a kind of vibration growing in her chest that gave her strength and dried her tears.

I'll call myself Dandelion Flower, she thought suddenly, *and Dandelion Flower will be my battle cry!*

She passed the back of her hand over her eyes and sniffed.

"You know something?" she said to the shepherdess, before setting off. "We've only just met, but I feel as if I love you like a sister."

"Have a good journey!" Maddalena said with a look of calm confidence.

"Have a good life!"

Jole mounted her horse and resumed her homeward journey.

5

S HE FOLLOWED THE TRAIL she had been along during the outward journey and, after a few hours, reached the dense wood further down the mountain, cloaked now in the light of sunset.

Only then did she feel a little safer.

But I'm sure that bastard is still hunting me. I must be careful.

All the same, amid this vast expanse of conifers, so dense and compact, a multitude of trees at least twenty metres high, she felt protected, like a child in the safe, warm arms of its own mother. She calmed down and her breathing slowed.

Coming to a stream, she filled the two canteens, and at last Samson, too, was able to drink.

She closed her eyes and after a few seconds opened them again, as if turning a page.

She felt almost as if she had reached safety. She thanked God and the stars, and the sun and the moon, and those majestic trees, and the clouds and the mountainsides and all creatures, since she, too, felt like a creature among many others.

She looked for and found a meadow in which she could spend the night. She gathered leaves and dry sticks from the undergrowth and with the help of a stone flint lit a small bonfire, fed with bigger and sturdier conifer branches that immediately crackled, scenting the air with fresh resin and dry wood.

She took from a bag the big piece of strong-smelling, sharp-tasting cheese that Maddalena had given her and ate a good half of it, putting what was left back in the bag.

Remembering the shepherdess, she took the dandelion flower from her ear and placed it delicately on her chest.

She lay down on the ground and covered herself with the blankets. Her back hurt, but she told herself that the pain would soon pass.

She listened to the majestic, disturbing sounds of nature.

In this life, everything is nothing. Prey and predators, souls that flee and other souls that pursue, souls that die and souls that kill. Everything is nothing, like clouds that form and a moment later are no more.

She heard the guttural, cavernous belling of the stags, a sound at once fascinating and frightening.

She heard the howling of wolves to the north.

She listened to an owl screeching.

She perceived, around her and in the surrounding meadow, the swarming and chirping of the nocturnal insects that had relieved the diurnal ones, tiny sentinels that have been alternating since the dawn of time, keeping watch over a world tormented by men.

The sky filled with stars: bright, beautiful and honest.

She wanted to weep, and she wept.

And it seemed to her as if even the firmament above her was weeping.

Then she fell asleep.

6

S HE SLEPT DEEPLY that night and woke late the following morning, when the sun was already high and shining in a blue sky cut across by a number of very high clouds that looked like scars. She opened her eyes and heard the gentle, rhythmically repeated sound of a chaffinch. The cries of thrushes and jays, some sweet, some sharp, also echoed through that patch of earth between the wood and the meadow. It was cold and the grass of the meadow was covered in a layer of dew.

She got laboriously to her feet. The pain had not passed. On the contrary: it was worse than it had been the previous evening.

She saw two hares in the middle of the little expanse in front of her.

They were in an erect position and were looking at each other as if exchanging confidences, perhaps even talking about her.

She yawned, stretched her arms and legs and ran her hands through her hair. She went to the bank of the stream and washed her face, then stripped quickly in order not to catch cold and washed her chest and legs. Each time she did this, she had the feeling that she was beautiful and seductive, along with the thought that nobody would ever marry her. Who could be interested in her, a poor peasant girl and smuggler?

She tied her long blonde mane of hair and put on her boots and the poncho she had made for herself by tearing into a blanket.

She sighed, and was walking slowly towards Samson, thinking of which direction to go in if she wanted to avoid further problems, when all at once she felt herself being hurled violently to the ground, face down. It only took a moment, and in that moment the black-clad man dragged her in silence for a few metres and finally turned her face up, aiming his rifle at her as he got back on his horse.

Jole brought him into focus. There was a gash on his face where the sharp stone had caught him, as well as streaks of dark blood on his forehead and temples, clotted in places.

"End of the road!" Mos cried.

She closed her eyes.

Nothing mattered any more. She sensed that this time there was no way out.

She thought about the little wooden horse and the dandelion flower she had in her pocket and cursed the fact that she had to die without being able to touch them and hug them to herself.

It seemed to her as if the world had suddenly turned purple.

The man cocked the rifle, and a moment later a loud shot echoed across the sky.

Dozens of birds rose in flight.

The shot echoed several times, bouncing between the trunks of the conifers and the walls of the surrounding mountains.

Jole managed to open her eyes, just enough to allow her to see Mos in front of her, with the rifle lowered, astride his black horse. He seemed to be motionless and in a strange position, as if bent over himself. A second later, she saw him bend even more and then collapse to the ground, stone dead.

Jole thought she was dreaming. She touched her head and arms and legs. She felt no pain.

She looked at herself: there was no trace of blood on her body. To her right, she made out a shadowy figure moving on the edge of the wood. She half-closed her eyes to see better: it was a man, and he was holding a smoking rifle still aimed at Mos. It was he who had fired the shot.

She tried to stand, but her breath failed her. Her nerves were in pieces and she felt an immense gratitude to this stranger, who with one shot from his rifle had killed her tormentor.

This tall, sturdy man came out of the wood with his rifle over his shoulder and she was able to see his face.

She was able to see, and recognize, the man who had saved her from certain death.

That man was Guglielmo, the charcoal burner.

He did not say anything. He went over to the man in black to make sure he was dead and then loaded him back on the same horse, now riderless, intending to take them both somewhere else.

"You're lucky," he said to her from a distance. "I never usually go this far from my pile to hunt."

She could not move a muscle. It was as if she were paralysed. This man must have been sent by God, it seemed to her.

"I was hunting nearby," he went on, coming towards her, still holding the reins of the black horse with Mos's body across the saddle.

She tried to say something, but all that emerged from her mouth was a weak "I can't... I can't..."

"You'll have time to thank me," he said, then, when he was close to her, "Take your horse and your things and follow me. You need a drink to perk you up."

Still incredulous and with her own death in her eyes, she summoned up the strength to move.

7

BEFORE GETTING TO THE CHARCOAL PILE, Guglielmo threw Mos's body from a nearby crag, in a place that was inaccessible and impossible to find except by the ravens, which immediately began to fly up into the sky, attracted by the carrion.

Then he shot a roebuck and loaded it on the black horse where the dead man had been.

He said not a single word while doing either thing, and Jole did not dare open her mouth.

A few hours later, when they got to the clearing in the centre of which was the charcoal pile, now well on its way and emitting smoke, Jole dismounted and Guglielmo began to skin and dismember the roebuck. When he had finished, he roasted two big pieces and put the rest away in a little hole that he himself had lately dug behind a promontory in the woods above.

In the meantime, the clouds that resembled long cuts and scars were swept away by the wind and the sky turned deep blue.

While Jole was at last eating meat and finally doing so in peace, savouring the taste of being alive and free, Guglielmo did not move from his enormous charcoal pile for a single moment.

The dome-shaped construction was at least four metres high and so large that it took a minute to go all the way around it. It was dark and covered in clay so tightly pressed that it looked like black mortar.

The broad layer of dry leaves under the topsoil could only be seen where there were air vents.

From these vents, dense, light-coloured smoke gradually emerged, heavy and scented with resinous bark, and rose slowly, undisturbed by the wind, protected by the tree trunks in the forests and by the mountains that enveloped the area. Guglielmo was working at the top of a ladder propped against the side of the pile.

He struck with the shovel, cleared the air vents with a long blackened stick and, when necessary, threw in firewood to bake the charcoal and make it "sing" its shrill song.

Guglielmo seemed not to sweat, moved no more than he needed to, and each blow he landed with the shovel ended up exactly where it was meant to, once and for all.

After a while, when he obviously knew that everything was going to be all right, at least for the time being, he came slowly down the ladder with the shovel in his hand, mopped his face and brow with a smoke-blackened handkerchief and knocked back a full swig of grappa.

Then he came over to Jole, holding the shovel in one hand and the bottle of grappa in the other.

Guglielmo was pleased to see her eat. He smiled at her. His face was much darker and more smoke-blackened than when she had seen him that first time. The whites of his eyes, veined with numerous red and yellow capillaries, stood out in that black but benevolent face.

"I don't know how to thank you," she said, removing with her teeth a piece of roebuck meat that was stubbornly sticking to the bone.

"You don't have to thank me."

"Seems like your work is going well," she said, indicating the big, smoking dome in the middle of the clearing.

He turned to look at the pile and gave a self-satisfied smile. "Yes, it is!"

"How much charcoal will you get out of it?"

"It's early to say, but I'd say a few quintals, if all goes well."

"How do you know when it's ready?"

Guglielmo took another swig of grappa. "When the first air vent lets out some nice dark smoke, that means the charcoal is ready. At that point, you need to take the pile down, cover the new charcoal with cold earth and put out the embers with a little water. But there's time. It's going to take another eight or ten days."

She wiped her mouth on the sleeve of her shirt.

"Why did that man want to kill you?" he suddenly asked her out of the blue.

"I don't know."

"I think you do."

"No, I don't."

"I understand," he said, dropping the subject. Deep down, he did not really care why that man had wanted to kill her, the important thing for him was that she was here now and she was all right. He knocked back the grappa and looked again at his charcoal pile. "And did you find what you were looking for?"

She snorted, gave a sad grimace, then drank water from the canteen and crossed her legs to be more comfortable, even though her lower back was still hurting her. "To find what I was looking for, I lost everything I believed in."

Guglielmo did not understand the meaning of these words, but accepted the answer anyway.

The sun had started to set, and from the woods the first gentle cries of the nightingales and the last exasperating tapping produced by the great spotted woodpecker both echoed.

She looked at the forest trees that encircled the clearing like an enclosure and for the first time had the feeling that she was in a kind of natural cage. It was a strange sensation.

She thought no more about it. Right now, she told herself, her one thought should be of sleeping. She would not move from here until the following day.

"To find what I was looking for, I lost everything I believed in," she repeated under her breath.

From her pockets, she took her little wooden horse and the sacred image of St Martin that had been her father's. She made sure Guglielmo did not see her do this, partly out of shyness and partly because these objects had a private meaning for her.

She stroked them surreptitiously, then placed them on the ground behind her back.

Guglielmo stood up, took the shovel and went and landed a sharp blow on a particular spot on the surface of the charcoal pile. Finally, he went for a few seconds inside the cabin of logs and branches he had built for himself as a night shelter and came back to her with another bottle in his hand, this one filled with a purple liquid.

"Now the only thing I want is to get home as soon as possible," Jole said.

"Of course," he said, drinking his grappa. "But for now it's best that you rest, that way you'll feel fresher when you leave tomorrow." He held the new bottle out to her, still untouched. "Blueberry and raspberry juice, it'll do you good."

She happily seized the bottle, opened it and took a decent mouthful. It was very satisfying. "You know, last night, when I camped out," she said, taking another swig, "I had no idea that man was going to sneak up on me like that. It may have been because I was nervous, or because I was tired, but I didn't think I could ever be caught by surprise."

Her head was starting to feel heavy, her hands growing increasingly numb.

She felt suddenly sleepy and had the impression she was seeing everything out of focus.

Finally, she felt herself growing weaker, ever weaker.

The charcoal burner smiled and after a few moments said, "Actually, I had a feeling you'd be back this way."

"Why?" Jole said, her voice little more than a whisper now.

"Because I was waiting for you."

And after these words he drank more grappa, while Jole fell into a deep sleep.

8

W HEN JOLE CAME TO, she had a splitting headache.
Her sight still seemed a little out of focus and her
limbs were still slightly numb. She was inside a little cave dug
out of the soft damp earth, fully clothed but bound hand and
foot and gagged.

She discerned a very strong smell of smoke and burning,
but could not work out where it was coming from.

She realized that evening and even night had passed, since
the sun's beams licking the edges of the entrance to this cave
had the colour and angle of dawn light.

The first thing she saw beside her was what was left of
the roebuck gutted and dismembered the day before, with its
stench of wild carrion and congealed blood.

She was alone and isolated, far from the rest of the world.

She did not think the huge man with kindly eyes who had
rescued her could have been responsible for reducing her to
this state. No, that was impossible.

But then, having by now completely regained her five
senses, she realized that the gag constricting her mouth was
that same smoke-blackened handkerchief the charcoal burner
had used to wipe the sweat from his brow as he worked. Then
she remembered that damned fruit juice he had given her.

God alone knew what he had put in it. *Where is he now?* she wondered.

She felt herself swoon with the pain, the discomfort and, last but not least, the terror.

Why had he done this to her? If he had wanted her copper and silver he could have robbed her and left it at that. What was the point of tying her up like a young goat and shutting her in here?

Jole despaired, but was unable to cry out her anguish.

She felt like a tree in the middle of a burning forest.

She felt like that roebuck beside her, like its remains, its dismembered flesh.

At that moment, she realized that she, too, had now fallen prey to the same fierce predator.

And after struggling for a few minutes, trying in vain to loosen the ropes that bound her wrists and ankles, she stopped moving and sank into a mood of total dejection. *Where is he now?* she wondered again.

In these last few days, she thought, there was one thing she had learnt, a simple but undeniable truth: that in life you should never trust anyone. And she thought about her mother, her brother and sister, who would never know what had happened to her, any more than they knew what had happened to her father. She had done nothing to deserve to die in this way, she thought, but above all, her family did not deserve this either.

They did not deserve a future like the one that awaited them, without a father and without the first-born, who had died God alone knew how, God alone knew when, God alone knew where or why. She felt guilty, because if she did not return they would continue to suffer the pains of hunger and poverty, which had decided to punish the De Boers for ever, poor damned victims of a vile, ungrateful fate.

She hoped one last time that the charcoal burner was not intending to run away and leave her to die of starvation in this hellish place, perhaps in the expectation that the wolves would come and eat her. *Where is he now?* she kept asking herself without getting an answer to the most disturbing question of her life.

9

As time passed, as the rays of the sun became bolder and less oblique, as the fetid odour of the carcass she had beside her rose into her nostrils together with the persistent smell of mould and damp that pervaded this place, as her strength ebbed from her, as her spirit faded and evaporated like dew in the May sun, Jole felt ever more lost.

She abandoned all hope.

He's robbed me of everything and abandoned me here, that much is sure.

10

ALL AT ONCE, the charcoal burner came back into the cave. She heard him muttering something incomprehensible and tried to turn towards him without, however, succeeding.

The man approached her with a torch in his hand and stopped a pace or two from her. His shadow was projected on the walls of the cave, turning his figure into that of a fearsome monster.

"Did you think I'd abandoned you?" he said, with a nasty laugh.

His voice was different from usual. It seemed to come from beyond the grave.

Jole felt herself die.

"Now I feel like enjoying myself, are you ready?" And he immediately turned serious. "I saw you yesterday morning, you know, at the stream, before that bastard arrived. I got a good look at you, I watched you as you washed, as you touched that body made by the angels…"

He reached out a brawny arm to her and in one move turned her around.

From this new position, Jole had a good view of the entrance to the cave and the light of the sun that was setting on the world, the same old world, a world that never changes from one day to the next. A world where only nature has respect for itself, even when it is cruel. A world where only the earth and the woods and the birds and the rocks and all the animals know the true sense of the sacred and preserve its fire for all eternity.

She could see the charcoal burner's big shovel propped against the wall of the cave, and the trees of the forest that seemed to be calling her back to them, laying claim to a kind of sincere fraternity.

The man bent over her, grunting and panting like a boar rooting about for food.

Suddenly a noise could be heard from outside.

A rustle of leaves and a muted neighing.

The man turned abruptly, pricking up his ears.

Samson, hobbled next to the other horse, could be heard whinnying briefly, as if alarmed by something.

The man leapt to his feet, cursing.

"I'll be right back," he said with a strange evil gleam in his eyes. "There's no rush, given that we're forced to be alone here for several days."

11

Left alone and bound in the dirt, Jole emitted a moan. Her mind started to wander.

The image of a dying Christ which she had seen as a little girl in the old Cluniac monastery of Campese came into her head. She had gone there with her grandmother Rosa to beg for mercy for her grandfather, who was being taken from them for ever by a terrible cough.

She recalled now the unease she had felt on looking at that figure. She was barely seven and had felt guilty about the pain that man had suffered in order to save *all* men, of all times and all races.

"But did he manage to save them all in the end?" she had asked her grandmother.

"Yes," the old woman had replied, holding the rosary in her hands.

A few months later, her grandfather had died anyway, and a year after that her grandmother had died, too, and Jole had never again gone back to that monastery at the entrance to the Brenta Valley.

Twelve years on, she felt like that Christ, with all the weight of the world on his back and all the pain but also all of men's resentment and anger and hatred transmuted into thorns and piercing his body.

She felt like that Christ.

12

THE CHARCOAL BURNER came back inside.

She had no idea how much time had passed. Her clear head and powers of reasoning had blurred until they were lost in a tangled forest of confused and unclear thoughts.

Have a few seconds passed? Have whole minutes passed? Half an hour? An hour? A day?

"It was nothing," the man said softly, as if to himself.

He advanced towards her where she lay defenceless on the ground, in exactly the same position in which he had left her.

He lifted her by her hair, and a strand came loose and fell to the ground, coming to rest on the tawny coat of what remained of the gutted roebuck.

He tore the handkerchief from her mouth and flung it away.

"Go on, scream, nobody's going to hear you!"

Jole said nothing. It was as if the man had managed to steal her voice, too, as well as her body and her soul.

"I told you to scream!" he cried. But still she remained silent and her eyes closed again in order to see the darkness, in order not to see anything, like when as a little girl she had played hide-and-seek with her sister and closed her eyes in order not to be seen, always ending up letting Antonia win. Now, too,

183

like a conditioned reflex, she played that game, knowing that she would lose everything.

The man slapped her, then again with the back of his hand. Loud slaps that echoed against the damp walls.

Then he looked at the rotting roebuck and exclaimed, "That damned stench!"

Still holding Jole by her long blonde hair, he dragged her outside, taking the shovel with him, too.

How long will it last? A few seconds? Whole minutes? Half an hour? An hour? A day?

He pulled her to within a few paces of the charcoal pile, where he flung the shovel down and threw her to the ground, face down. Then he grabbed a bottle of grappa and took a sizeable swig.

At that moment, he heard a strange noise behind him. He stopped and looked around.

"There's something not right here." He again grabbed Jole and took her back inside the cave.

The following afternoon, he returned. He again grabbed her by the hair and took her back out to the *jal*, the clearing where he had built his charcoal pile. There were no clouds, no birds in flight. Even though his breath already stank of grappa, he continued drinking. He looked around with a mocking sneer.

"How do you like my pile?" he asked her, his eyes steeped in madness.

She managed to turn her face just enough to keep breathing,

even though what entered her nostrils was the dust of the clearing and the ash that emerged from the charcoal pile and settled on the ground, covering it in grey snow. She had the taste of blood on her lips and inside her mouth.

To her right, not far away, she glimpsed the two horses, hers and the black one, both tied.

Samson was nervous and very restless. Harnessed as always, with all her things on it.

He kept moving, biting the rope that tied him tightly to a birch and kicking without any hope of freeing himself. Jole was confused, her vision faltering, yet it seemed to her that against the trunk of the pine behind the two horses, where all three rifles—the charcoal burner's, Mos's and hers—had been propped the previous evening, there were now only two. Her blurred eyes recognized Mos's and the charcoal burner's, but not hers. Not her St Paul.

"Listen to me when I speak to you!" the charcoal burner cried, bringing Jole's mind back to that hell. He drank some more and then, apparently calmer, said, "So, how do you like it? Look how beautiful it is. You need love to make them like that, you know? You need passion, like in all things."

She did not emit a single word, but she could feel tears gushing from her eyes, streaking her face and mixing with the blood and the dust and the ash.

I think I'm dead.

He bent over her and with two abrupt gestures filled with brute force tore off first her trousers, then her shirt, and flung them a short distance.

He took her by the abdomen, lifted her and made her kneel.

I believe I'm dead.

"Let me feel…" he said, touching her breasts from behind with a smoke-blackened hand, while with his other hand he pulled his trousers down to his ankles.

Then he stopped groping her and slid the same hand between her legs.

I hope I'm dead.

"Here I am!" the charcoal burner said, beginning to bend clumsily over her back.

13

"STOP OR I SHOOT, devil's spawn!"

On his knees, the charcoal burner froze.

What he heard from behind his back was an unknown voice, rough and filled with hatred.

"Get up and turn around!" the voice cried harshly.

"Jole!" it next cried.

It can't be.

14

THE CHARCOAL BURNER tried to get to his feet with his hands up, but drunk and heavy as he was he fell to the ground, landing on his back.

"Jole, it's me!" the man with the rifle cried.

I must be dead, Jole thought.

It only took a few seconds.

Keeping the rifle trained on the charcoal burner, the man took a few steps forward, dragging one leg. He approached the giant lying on his back on the ground and the almost lifeless girl.

When he saw the stranger in front of him, the charcoal burner closed his eyes.

The man with the rifle spat in his black and ruddy face with all the contempt that might have been lurking in his heart, then hit him hard several times with the butt of the rifle, both in the face and in the genitals.

"Take that, you bastard!" he cried, hitting him high and low.

It can't be.

"You whore's son!" And he kicked him in the ribs.

"May Satan carry you away!" Another blow in the face.

It can't be him.

After a few minutes, he pulled up the rifle and ran as best he could to Jole.

"Papà!"

"Jole!" he said, throwing himself desperately on his daughter.

"Pà…" She could barely manage a sigh, her voice almost gone.

The charcoal burner was lying on the ground, his face like an enormous tomato that has fallen from a cliff, his mouth bubbling with red foam and deathlike sounds.

Augusto De Boer pulled a knife from his waist and cut the ropes binding her wrists and ankles, then took off his fustian jacket and was wrapping it around her chest when the charcoal burner, who had in the meantime somehow managed to get to his feet, landed him a blow on the back with the shovel.

Augusto fell to the ground, stunned, and instantaneously his daughter once again saw the charcoal burner looming over her.

Dandelion Flower is my battle cry, she thought.

Still lying on the ground, she found within herself a strength she did not know she had.

She quickly reached out a hand, grabbed the rifle, aimed it at his head and pressed the trigger.

She fired as if there in front of her was not only that monstrous tormentor, but all the tormentors in the world, all the most repulsive men on the face of the earth, but also all the cruelties of life, her and her family's misfortunes, the injustices to which they had always been subjected, the oppression, the suffering, the days of hunger and pain and toil and humiliation.

She fired at all that, thinking she could wipe out everything with a rifle shot.

The reverberation was massive.

From the surrounding forest myriads of birds rose in flight, startled by that sudden, terrifying roar.

The echo of the shot spread through the valleys and bounced off the walls of the Vette Feltrine and returned to the clearing as a chilling vibration.

A secret tremor passed through Jole's blood, a mixture of pain and revenge. It was as if she had freed herself from anguish. While the sound of the rifle shot echoed in her head, seemingly unwilling to leave her ears, dark, blurred images of her childhood came into her mind, like when she had first heard the big bells of the church in Asiago ringing for the dead or when she had heard women singing at her grandmother's funeral.

In both situations, she had been forced to cover her ears so as not to hear a sound that evoked grief.

The whole of the adventure she had lived through in the last few days passed in front of her and she felt faint. But she forced herself to remain alert, because her eyes wanted to see everything so that she could carry it within her.

She lay still, looking up at that huge man. There was an opening in his head, but for a moment he still stood there, not moving.

Damn.

She fired straight at his head.

She hit him in the face.

I've killed him.

The charcoal burner fell to the ground.

I've killed him. For ever.

15

A UGUSTO AND HIS DAUGHTER sat in silence by the fire, half an hour's walk from the place where they had found each other again after years of separation. They were in a daze, like two mountain men who have escaped a devastating landslide. To shield herself from the cold, Jole had wrapped herself in a blue blanket that had belonged to her victim.

It was late in the afternoon of the same day, the day on which Jole had been reunited with her father and killed a man. The day on which she had turned from a victim into a murderer.

After shooting the charcoal burner, Jole had gone to tend to her father. She had approached him with awe and reverence, incredulous at seeing him there in front of her. She had stood motionless for a moment or two, contemplating those features she knew so well, features she had thought she would never see again. Then, as if waking from a dream, she had felt his pulse, touched his brow, checked that he was breathing. Luckily, he had only fainted. After a few minutes, he had opened his eyes and sat up.

"We're safe," he had said, when he had got to his feet and seen the charcoal burner's body. He had immediately embraced his daughter.

They had agreed that the best thing to do was to abandon that place in haste, but that first of all they would have to hide or get rid of the charcoal burner's body. Jole had suggested leaving it in the cave where she had been confined, but her father had decided to shove it into the lighted charcoal pile, letting it disintegrate for ever in the man's own creation. And they had done so: they had made a big enough gap in the surface of the pile to get at least part of the corpse through and then pushed him inside with what little strength remained to them.

They rested by the fire and ate everything they had managed to steal from the charcoal burner's cabin, including bacon rinds, rye bread and Lamon beans.

Augusto had a voracious appetite, whereas Jole felt as if her stomach were blocked. She would put the food in her mouth and chew it for a long time without swallowing.

A few paces away, Samson and the black horse were hobbled to an oak but had sufficient rope to graze on the last yellowed grass of autumn and to drink from the little stream that flowed past them.

"Don't think about it. You did what you had to do, Jole… although I should have been the one to do it."

Jole stared into space, holding in her hand the wilted, poor-looking dandelion flower that Maddalena had given her.

You're in as bad a shape as I am, she thought, observing it with compassion as she turned it in her fingers.

Her blue, green and grey eyes were like an Alpine glacier weary of the endless cold and anxious to become a summer lake.

Augusto chewed bacon rind and beans and looked around suspiciously, like a stag in the middle of a meadow.

He had changed. He was even thinner than he had been before, he was lame in one leg and his moustache had become one with his long grey beard.

"Why were you there?" he asked her.

She returned to reality and looked at him. "I was on my way home."

"You should never have left."

"Someone had to. We all thought you were dead, Papà. What happened to you?"

He was silent for a moment, and for the first time Jole saw a tear run down his cheek.

"I've been wandering about. I had to hide."

Jole's eyes opened wide. "So you did kill that girl?"

"Is that what they told you? The bastards." Augusto lowered his eyes and sighed. "Everyone down in the inn knew that half-mad Kraut, Näckler, killed the girl. But to save him, De Menech told the customs men to look for an Italian. He claimed he'd seen me kill her, but it was a complete lie. We'd had an argument the day before: I'd found someone who was offering me much more silver and copper than that shark. I'd gone to him and told him this would be the last load I brought him, and he started insulting me, he was even on the point of grabbing his rifle. And so within a few hours I found myself running away from Imer, forced to escape from the emperor's officers not just as a smuggler, but as a rapist and murderer."

She had never heard him speak so quickly. He seemed like a different man. There are some things that change men for ever.

"So you didn't kill her!" Jole said, relieved.

Augusto grunted a "No" as sharp as his face and looked her straight in the eyes. "The very idea of killing a girl like you or Antonia makes me sick. I wouldn't wish it on my worst enemy!"

Then he told her about his escape from the customs men and the long climb back through the Noana Valley and up Mount Pavione, where the *Zollwache* had caught up with him and shot him in the leg.

"With a bloody knee, I managed to cross the border on Mount Pavione and come down the other side."

"And then?"

"I bandaged my wound and treated it as best I could with plants, then dragged myself across the south side of the Vette Feltrine until I met some woodcutters, may God protect them always, who tended me and took me to their cabin... I thought of all of you... all the time..."

Augusto was silent for a moment and looked at his daughter with watery eyes. Then he threw another log onto the crackling fire and dozens of incandescent sparks rose into the air.

"Papà..." she said, going to him and embracing him. They remained in this embrace for a long time, then he continued, "After tending to me, one of them, Tomaso, carried me on his back to his house in Laredo, a hamlet of three houses hidden in the woods above Lasen. There, his wife and sister-in-law immediately took care of me, even though I didn't have much expectation of being saved, with a crushed knee and tibia and the wound already infected."

"Why did they trust a fugitive?"

"I don't know if they believed what I told them. But I know what compassion and mercy are. Especially among those at the bottom of the heap."

She ran a hand through her greasy, darkened hair and gestured to him to continue.

"I was close to death, but they didn't abandon me. I had a high fever for two weeks, then gradually recovered, but didn't get out of bed for the first time until I'd been there for four months. Tomaso had made me a crutch to walk on. I'd lost more than ten kilos and wasn't eating anything. A year later I began walking again, with a limp, and it was only after a year and a half that I started to get my weight and strength back. From then on, I prepared myself for going home. Every day I went for walks in the woods, longer ones each day, to exercise my breathing and my leg. I had only one thought in my head: going home. Going back to my family."

"And we thought you were dead…"

Augusto's eyes again grew moist. "That was my biggest sorrow. I couldn't inform you, couldn't let you know how I was. And so, when a week ago I realized I was ready to leave Tomaso's family and go home, I felt like the happiest man in the world."

"What about the mule, Hector?"

"Killed on Mount Pavione by the *Zollwache*'s bullets, poor beast."

"Poor thing… And how did you find me?"

"After two days of walking, it was getting to be really hard. I'd got it into my head to do one thing before going home, but I realized I didn't have the strength to carry it out. Luckily, on the slopes of Mount Pavione, which is where I was, I met a young shepherdess."

"A shepherdess? Was she by any chance wearing a hat with a fox's tail?"

"Yes."

"She tended to me, too."

"I know. She told me she'd met a beautiful young blonde girl from the Brenta Valley who was running away. She gave me your name. I told her I was your father. I summoned up all the strength I could find in me and set off to look for you."

"I should have found you, and instead you found me. But how did you know where I was?"

Augusto put a hand in his pocket and moved it about as if trying to clutch hold of something. "I got to the charcoal pile almost by chance, because I'd seen the smoke from a distance above the trees. Reaching the clearing where the two horses were tied, I found these on the ground!"

And he held out to her the little wooden horse and the sacred image of St Martin that she had left on the ground before drinking the juice that had knocked her out.

"Then I recognized St Paul propped against a tree. I took it, checked it was loaded, and just then I saw him dragging you across the clearing—"

"Enough!"

Almost without realizing it, Jole had screamed. Every word or image that reminded her of the recent past was hateful to her.

Father and daughter lapsed into silence. Above them, the waning moon looked melancholy, while the stars shone so brightly they seemed alive and alert to their words, as if trying to understand their secrets and seal them for ever in the crystalline autumn sky.

"How big you've grown, Jole!" Augusto said at last, unable to take his eyes off his daughter.

She lowered her eyes and clung to him.

She had been telling herself for a long time that he was dead, but in her heart of hearts she had never stopped dreaming of this moment. She had not seen him, had not heard his voice for three years, and now she burst into tears from the emotion.

It was as if her father had died and then been reborn, come back miraculously to life. But it was as if she, too, had come back to life. It was a strange sensation: to be born again with her own father, together at the same moment.

Augusto, in the meantime, was fantasizing about his return home, silently talking to his family. *How I miss you, Sergio, with your little wooden horses, your curious eyes, your frail little hands,* he was thinking. *I miss when you come to me and sit on my knees because someone has shouted at you, or else because nobody can spare the time to be with you. I love you. Hold on, Sergio, soon I'll be with you and Antonia and your mother. Soon I'll be with all of you.* It was only now that he realized he had not asked Jole any questions about his family. Thinking about them so much had made them seem close.

"How is your mother?" he asked. "And Antonia? And Sergio?"

Sobbing, Jole wiped her tears. "When we get home they'll be fine. They'll be fine."

"Why did you do it? Why did you set off for the Primiero Valley on your own?"

"I told you. At home we suffer hunger, as you know. And since you left, it's been even worse, much worse…"

"I know."

They ate more bacon grilled on the fire and rye bread.

"I've earned four kilos of silver and eight of copper," Jole said after a while, in an outburst of pride.

Astonished at this news, Augusto abruptly spat out something he had in his mouth. "Are you joking?"

"No, it's true," she said, unfazed.

"May God bless you, daughter!"

But sad she was and sad she remained.

And when she recounted her whole adventure, he was astounded. "So that black horse belongs to the man who was hunting me, too?"

"Yes."

Luckily for them, it was a docile, submissive nag.

"What about the other one?"

She told him the story of her Haflinger, and this time they both fell silent for a long time.

Augusto was lost in thought. He was thinking about his family, about those long years, the people who had helped him. And after a while he could not tell if he had said what he was thinking out loud or only to himself.

16

"L ET'S GO HOME, PAPÀ!"

Augusto looked at the moon, embraced his daughter, who was sitting beside him, and then moved his lips imperceptibly, as if trying to recite a prayer without being heard.

"Let's go home!" Jole repeated.

"Yes. But first there are two things we have to do. The last two."

At this point she abruptly pulled away from him and looked at him as one looks at a madman.

"And to do them we have to go back to Mount Pavione," he went on, still looking at the moon.

Jole leapt to her feet. "I'm not going back to Mount Pavione!" she said.

17

At dawn the following morning, they quickly rode back up through the conifer forest on the two horses and in less than three hours reached the south side of Mount Pavione.

Jole had wept for much of the previous evening before collapsing into sleep. This morning, though, she had woken different.

Opening her eyes, she had felt better. She had listened to the song of the blackbirds and thrushes and had interpreted it as a calm invitation to leave, to follow her father.

After all that had happened, the idea of retracing her steps, going back over her open wounds, did not appeal to her at all and required a great sacrifice, but the fact that it was her father who was asking it of her, this man she had mourned for two years and had now finally found again, persuaded her. Augusto had also told her that she would soon understand the importance of this decision.

She realized she would do anything not to lose him again before they got home.

And so she put her hat on her head and mounted Samson with her rifle, the weapon that had saved her from death, even though it had changed her life.

They were both exhausted and conscious that this variation in their return journey would represent a great risk, both because of their physical condition, and because they might encounter customs officers on the way.

Sitting on their horses, they looked up at the summit of the great mountain. The peak had turned white since they had last seen it and an impressive wind was blowing the first dusting of snow through the air.

"Follow me!" he said.

For a while, they climbed up through the prairies that crowned the massif and then, when the slope grew hard and tiring, followed unlikely paths and directions improvised by Augusto, who constantly looked around to intercept possible dangers.

After more than half an hour of steep climbing, the wind started up, that wind that Jole had by now got to know and respect, submitting almost humbly to its powerful voice.

That soul of the border to which her father himself had introduced her, teaching her to recognize its deep voice.

"Everything all right?" he asked.

"Yes!"

They looked at one another and understood. Augusto pointed at a group of Swiss pines and moved in that direction.

She followed, remaining always close to him.

Before long, having passed the last pines in that part of the scree, pines bent by the constant wind, Augusto dismounted, tied his horse to one of the trees and proceeded on foot, motioning to his daughter to do the same.

With difficulty, they crossed an area of large grey stones and at last came within sight of an old landslide. Jole shuddered: the smallest rock was as big as a cow. Augusto looked around to get his bearings, then limped ten paces further down and pointed to a large boulder.

Jole joined her father and looked at the boulder. On it, the letters ADB had been carved with a white stone.

From the way Augusto's beard and moustache moved, she knew that he was laughing. She definitely saw his eyes light up with joy.

Without wasting any time, he bent down—it was not easy, thanks to the leg he could not move—and began to remove all the smallest stones from the base of the rock.

"Give me a hand!" he said, looking up at her.

Jole, too, bent and began lifting all the stones she could find, until she saw a piece of jute sticking out.

"This is it!" Augusto cried with excitement. "We've done it."

After a few minutes, the piece of jute proved to be an actual sack. A large, full sack.

Augusto took his knife, made a cut in the sack and slipped a hand inside.

A moment later, the hand came back out clutching the barrel of a rifle, which could gradually be seen in its entirety.

"Have you ever seen St Paul without St Peter?" he said, passing her the Werndl-Holub that was the twin of her own.

She laughed.

Augusto stuck his arm into the ground and continued looking for something else until his face changed expression again.

A moment or two later, he pulled out, one at a time, five kilos of silver and seven of copper and passed them to Jole who could not believe her eyes.

When at last he took out the eighth bar of copper, he said, "I told you it was worth it. They're all here, five plus eight. Added to yours, that makes nine kilos of silver and sixteen of copper."

"But when did you hide them?" Jole asked, struggling to put them all in the rucksack.

"When they shot Hector, I gathered them all up and took them with me."

"With a wounded leg?"

"With a wounded leg. I crossed the mountain and deposited them here. Then I went down into the woods over towards Lasen."

"Papà," she said, looking around, stunned by the ruggedness of this place, "how did you manage to—"

"The soul of the border, daughter. The soul of the border helped me!"

She helped him to his feet and they slowly went back to the horses.

"Does this mean we're finished with smuggling, Papà?" she asked before mounting her horse.

"Yes, but this is not all ours."

"Why?"

"God would never forgive me if I didn't repay the man who saved me." And taking the reins of his horse, he added in a peremptory tone, "To Laredo. Follow me!"

And he began to descend towards the valley, in a north-easterly direction, while the soul of the border blew loudly, howling bitter words of anger, vengeance and justice.

18

THEY DESCENDED A SLOPE that only Augusto knew, on the lookout as always for the presence of patrols, given their continued proximity to the border. They went forward as if charged with a mission whose origins lay in the remote past, as if bound by a blood pact to an implacable ancient order.

They rode through conifer woods and then, further down, stretches of oaks and broad beeches.

After riding for three hours, remaining always at altitude, amid constant rises and falls, perilous descents and steep ascents, the De Boers came to a cabin built from larch trunks. In the front yard, just under a large wild mulberry tree, was a tall, sturdy man in his fifties, busy chopping firewood into large logs ready to be stockpiled for burning in the stove during the winter. He moved at a steady rhythm, repeating the same movements, as if destined to perform these gestures all his life.

Augusto and Jole rode across the meadow, and when they were some twenty metres from the cabin, the man saw them, stopped chopping, leant on the handle of the axe and watched them as if trying to work out who they were.

"Tomaso!" Augusto cried, raising his arm.

The man gave a smile that changed the colour of his face and immediately came walking towards the two of them.

"Have you changed your mind? On a horse? And who's she?" he asked, casting a curious look at the girl by Augusto's side.

"She's my daughter," Augusto said, dismounting.

Tomaso went and called his wife, his mother-in-law and the children, two irrepressible boys of eight and six. They all embraced, put the horses in the barn and entered the cabin.

Tomaso's family were poor, like the De Boers, and poverty was the language that united them, that led them to say and hear the same things, to feel the very same sufferings and torments of life.

They had little food, but they shared it among everyone. They ate a little bread and barley soup and drank water mixed with raspberry and elderberry spirits.

While Jole amused herself playing with the two children, Augusto told Tomaso what had happened and how he had been reunited with his daughter, who said goodbye to the two little imps and sat down again at the table next to her father. Her back still hurt, but that was nothing now.

Then her father asked her to bring him the rucksack and she handed it to him.

Augusto took out three kilos of silver and put them on the old spruce table. "These are for you, as a mark of gratitude. Without your help, I wouldn't be here with my daughter."

Tomaso's eyes suddenly opened wide, then closed again. "We can't accept that!" he replied promptly.

"You have to. In the name of our friendship."

Unaccustomed to receiving gifts, Tomaso bowed his head. Then he stood up and clasped Augusto in an embrace, the universal mark of affection and gratitude.

After a few moments, Augusto looked at his daughter and said:

"Now we can go home."

19

THEY TRAVELLED FOR THREE DAYS.

Three days of exertion and impatience, during which Jole felt changed for ever.

In those few days away from home many things had happened to her, much more than had ever happened to her before. She was not only exhausted, she had lost weight, she was dirty, made rough and wild by the sun and the night and the wind, and her muscles and nerves were in pieces.

She was confused in her feelings, but right now the one that prevailed was happiness. She was going home, back to her mother and siblings, and above all she was going back there together with her father, carrying the future in the form of coarse, shapeless bars crammed into her rucksack. And that was a lot.

They crossed the beech woods and oak woods of Lasen, again tackled the slopes of Mount Pavione, which they greeted as if it were a kind of high altar, penetrated the infinite expanses of conifer forest that led from the Vette Feltrine to up above Fonzaso, keeping themselves always at altitude and at a due distance even from the smallest towns and villages. They hunted for hares and fished for trout.

They passed lakes, looked at streams, rode through meadows and stretches of yellowed pastures and over hills of broad-leaved trees now stripped of their foliage. They looked down at the town of Arsiè from up above in the woods, then plunged into the mountains on the left-hand side of the Brenta.

They descended the steep slope that led down the mountainside, heard the whistle of the new locomotive echo through the great valley, crossed their sacred river and climbed the slope on the right-hand side of the Brenta, towards the Asiago plateau, moved along tracks and paths and lanes first opened up by Augusto, and at last came to the first *masiere* of tobacco.

Augusto almost always rode in front and Jole would keep ten metres behind. Sometimes, though, they proceeded side by side, and at other times it was Jole who led the way.

At the end of the third day they reached Nevada.

Before leaving the dense, thorny wood that had led them to their house, Augusto said to her, "Go, it should be you." And he let her pass in front of him so that she should arrive first.

When Jole saw the walls of her abode, she loosened the red kerchief she wore around her neck and burst into tears.

It seemed to her that she had been away for months, years. And, as far as she was concerned, she really had been.

They left the horses in the meadow in front of the old farmhouse and walked towards the *meléster*, the mountain ash, on which only a handful of orange-coloured berries still remained.

Reaching the tree, they heard the cries of joy of their nearest and dearest, and then saw them run out with open arms.

Agnese embraced her husband and daughter and knelt to thank God, weeping with joy.

Antonia and Sergio went crazy with happiness.

Once they had entered the house, Jole and her father realized that they had a fever. The strains of the journey and the tiredness that remained in their damp, fatigue-cracked bones, bones that had several times seen death and at last again life, had reduced them to a sorry state.

"Here, Papà," Jole said, giving him back his rifle. "I don't ever want to see it again."

Augusto took it from her hands and hid it for ever alongside St Peter.

He, too, wanted nothing more to do with it.

A few days later, when they had recovered, Augusto hid the silver and copper in safe places, then rearranged the shed for the two new horses and began mending everything that had rather been left to its own devices in the last few years, including the roof of the house, through which rainwater had started to percolate.

Then he retook possession of the *masiere* and put order back into many of the things that had been neglected in his absence.

20

DURING THE FIRST DAYS after her return, Jole spent much time alone, in silence. She felt a kind of inner darkness. She wanted to understand herself. She would walk through the woods barefoot, as she had done as a little girl, planting the soles of her feet now on the sharp brushwood, now on the soft, spongy moss. Through this direct contact with the earth, she felt as if she were becoming a nymph, she felt at one with the woods. Sometimes she would sit down on a rock and listen with eyes closed to the cries of the blue tits and the long-tailed tits and imagine that she was jumping from branch to branch of the highest spruces, just like those little birds. Then she would dream of opening her arms and flying away, soaring between the earth and the sky. The song of the birds made her feel good, as did contact with the trees. Every now and again she would embrace one, clinging as tightly as she could to its hard bark, taking strength from it. Strength and serenity. Then she would sigh and resume walking, gathering a few late flowers, or a few pine cones. Once she even found an eagle's feather.

Five days after her return, with pride and tenderness, she showed Sergio her little wooden horse and told him it had been of great help and comfort to her. That evening, she went to recover the dandelion that the mysterious shepherdess had given her. She had hidden it in the woodshed the day she had returned home, placing it among the logs of Alpine maple. She was convinced she would find it more wilted and faded, perhaps even rotted away. Instead, the flower was much yellower, healthier and more beautiful than when she had left it a few days earlier. It was as if it had been reborn.

Jole could not believe her eyes. She carefully picked it up and ran into the house. She took the heavy Bible from her parents' room, opened it and put the flower inside it, placing it delicately between the pages of the Wisdom of Solomon, which was more or less halfway through, and closed the book. Thus pressed, the flower would be preserved in a dry state for ever.

I'll make a beautiful charm or pendant out of it! she thought with a smile. *My sister will teach me how to coat it in spruce resin, and I'll create a magnificent pendant!*

21

A GNESE THANKED GOD for a whole week, praying every hour of every day. After seven days, when she was able to get back to looking after her children, Augusto went down to Bassano del Grappa with a small part of their treasure. Jole asked if she could go with him, but he had said no, he would go alone.

The following day, he returned with a huge cart crammed with food—sacks of beans, salt, sugar, flour, pulses, maize—and even a number of animals, including eight chicks, a rooster, ten hens and two kids. There was also leather and some fabrics.

Two weeks later, he went down again and brought home two Burlina heifers and three piglets.

For the rest, everything went back to being more or less the way it had been before, except that for a while life was better for De Boers, although they were still poor mountain peasants, servants of the Royal Tobacco Company and of the land, and they still lived in constant awareness of the inevitable arrival of one famine then another, one misfortune after another, one war followed by another.

22

A UGUSTO NEVER AGAIN thought of smuggling tobacco, and nor of course did his daughter.

Both kept silent about what had happened to them, and the others never asked them any questions.

Before long, Jole's beauty once again shone forth like that of a Dolomite undine, even though there remained a melancholy light in her eyes, something that had no name, no voice, no colour, and yet dwelt in her like a vague memory or a dream never dreamt.

That extraordinary adventure had tested her, made her adult before her time and shown her the most terrible aspects of the world and men and life.

Augusto again stopped speaking and resumed chewing tobacco. That magnificent tobacco for which the people of other lands beyond the border were ready to do anything.

Then came winter and the cold and with them the first great snowfalls, which cloaked Nevada and the uplands in a deep white blanket.

And everything fell silent.

It was the end of 1896.

For a few more years, the border with Austria remained where it was, where father and daughter had known it, crossed it and challenged it many times, where the wind of altitude and injustice blew, where Jole had heard the deep, disquieting voice of its soul, where men confronted and killed each other.

Where, above all, she had learnt to know the deep meaning of the border, that border that has always clearly divided the world into crowns of gold and crowns of thorns, into the powerful and the poor.

But more than anything, she had learnt to know a deeper, more private border, the thin border that separates good from evil, the invisible line of demarcation between reason and madness that is hidden in every human heart, transforming angels into demons and demons into angels.

Whereas, way up here, the expanses of grass and the stones and the dandelions would continue to know nothing about any border.

And Jole continued in the same way, in imitation of the nature she loved so much, hoping privately that one day nobody would have to feel, one way or another, like a stranger.

Either in her mountains, or in this world.

Author's Note

In the planning of this novel, I found valuable inspiration in a number of sources, including *Storia di Tönle* by Mario Rigoni Stern and *La strada delle piccole Dolomiti* by Arturo Zanuso.

The description of the charcoal pile on pp. 171–3 owes a lot to Pietro Parolin and his book *Saltaboschi* (Panda edizioni, 2016).

Pushkin Press

Pushkin Press was founded in 1997, and publishes novels, essays, memoirs, children's books—everything from timeless classics to the urgent and contemporary.

Our books represent exciting, high-quality writing from around the world: we publish some of the twentieth century's most widely acclaimed, brilliant authors such as Stefan Zweig, Marcel Aymé, Teffi, Antal Szerb, Gaito Gazdanov and Yasushi Inoue, as well as compelling and award-winning contemporary writers, including Andrés Neuman, Edith Pearlman, Eka Kurniawan, Ayelet Gundar-Goshen and Chigozie Obioma.

Pushkin Press publishes the world's best stories, to be read and read again. To discover more, visit www.pushkinpress.com.

═══

THE SPECTRE OF ALEXANDER WOLF

GAITO GAZDANOV

'A mesmerising work of literature' Antony Beevor

SUMMER BEFORE THE DARK

VOLKER WEIDERMANN

'For such a slim book to convey with such poignancy the extinction of a generation of "Great Europeans" is a triumph' *Sunday Telegraph*

MESSAGES FROM A LOST WORLD

STEFAN ZWEIG

'At a time of monetary crisis and political disorder… Zweig's celebration of the brotherhood of peoples reminds us that there is another way' *The Nation*

THE EVENINGS

GERARD REVE

'Not only a masterpiece but a cornerstone manqué of modern European literature' Tim Parks, *Guardian*

BINOCULAR VISION

EDITH PEARLMAN

'A genius of the short story' Mark Lawson, *Guardian*

IN THE BEGINNING WAS THE SEA

TOMÁS GONZÁLEZ

'Smoothly intriguing narrative, with its touches of sinister, Patricia Highsmith-like menace' *Irish Times*

BEWARE OF PITY

STEFAN ZWEIG

'Zweig's fictional masterpiece' *Guardian*

THE ENCOUNTER

PETRU POPESCU

'A book that suggests new ways of looking at the world and our place within it' *Sunday Telegraph*

WAKE UP, SIR!

JONATHAN AMES

'The novel is extremely funny but it is also sad and poignant, and almost incredibly clever' *Guardian*

THE WORLD OF YESTERDAY

STEFAN ZWEIG

'*The World of Yesterday* is one of the greatest memoirs of the twentieth century, as perfect in its evocation of the world Zweig loved, as it is in its portrayal of how that world was destroyed' David Hare

WAKING LIONS

AYELET GUNDAR-GOSHEN

'A literary thriller that is used as a vehicle to explore big moral issues. I loved everything about it' *Daily Mail*

FOR A LITTLE WHILE

RICK BASS

'Bass is, hands down, a master of the short form, creating in a few pages a natural world of mythic proportions' *New York Times Book Review*

JOURNEY BY MOONLIGHT
ANTAL SZERB

'Just divine… makes you imagine the author has had private access to your own soul' Nicholas Lezard, *Guardian*

BEFORE THE FEAST
SAŠA STANIŠIĆ

'Exceptional… cleverly done, and so mesmerising from the off… thought-provoking and energetic' *Big Issue*

A SIMPLE STORY
LEILA GUERRIERO

'An epic of noble proportions… [Guerriero] is a mistress of the telling phrase or the revealing detail' *Spectator*

FORTUNES OF FRANCE
ROBERT MERLE

1 *The Brethren*
2 *City of Wisdom and Blood*
3 *Heretic Dawn*

'Swashbuckling historical fiction' *Guardian*

TRAVELLER OF THE CENTURY
ANDRÉS NEUMAN

'A beautiful, accomplished novel: as ambitious as it is generous, as moving as it is smart' Juan Gabriel Vásquez, *Guardian*

A WORLD GONE MAD
ASTRID LINDGREN

'A remarkable portrait of domestic life in a country maintaining a fragile peace while war raged all around' *New Statesman*

MIRROR, SHOULDER, SIGNAL
DORTHE NORS

'Dorthe Nors is fantastic!' Junot Díaz

RED LOVE: THE STORY OF AN EAST GERMAN FAMILY
MAXIM LEO

'Beautiful and supremely touching… an unbearably poignant description of a world that no longer exists' *Sunday Telegraph*

THE BEAUTIFUL BUREAUCRAT

HELEN PHILLIPS

'Funny, sad, scary and beautiful. I love it' Ursula K. Le Guin

THE RABBIT BACK LITERATURE SOCIETY

PASI ILMARI JÄÄSKELÄINEN

'Wonderfully knotty… a very grown-up fantasy masquerading as
quirky fable. Unexpected, thrilling and absurd' *Sunday Telegraph*

BEAUTY IS A WOUND

EKA KURNIAWAN

'An unforgettable all-encompassing epic' *Publishers Weekly*

BARCELONA SHADOWS

MARC PASTOR

'As gruesome as it is gripping… the writing is extraordinarily
vivid… Highly recommended' *Independent*

MEMORIES—FROM MOSCOW TO THE BLACK SEA

TEFFI

'Wonderfully idiosyncratic, coolly heartfelt and
memorable' William Boyd, *Sunday Times*

WHILE THE GODS WERE SLEEPING

ERWIN MORTIER

'A monumental, phenomenal book' *De Morgen*

BUTTERFLIES IN NOVEMBER

AUÐUR AVA ÓLAFSDÓTTIR

'A funny, moving and occasionally bizarre exploration of
life's upheavals and reversals' *Financial Times*

BY BLOOD

ELLEN ULLMAN

'Delicious and intriguing' *Daily Telegraph*

THE LAST DAYS

LAURENT SEKSIK

'Mesmerising… Seksik's portrait of Zweig's final months
is dignified and tender' *Financial Times*